Twelve
Twelve i
One **UNIFO**

Harlequin Blaze's bestselling miniseries
continues with another year of irresistible soldiers
from all branches of the armed forces.

Don't miss

MISSION: SEDUCTION
by Candace Havens
September 2013

COMMAND PERFORMANCE
by Sara Jane Stone
October 2013

BACK IN SERVICE
by Isabel Sharpe
November 2013

A SOLDIER'S CHRISTMAS
by Leslie Kelly, Joanne Rock and Karen Foley
December 2013

Uniformly Hot!
The Few. The Proud. The Sexy as Hell.

Available wherever Harlequin books are sold.

Dear Reader,

We first met Lieutenant Rafe McCawley when he helped out his best friend, Captain Will, in *Model Marine*. I fell in love with Rafe in that story. He's funny, strong and does what it takes to get the job done. What you may not know is when Will was injured that last time, so was Rafe. His recovery takes him to Fiji, where he meets a pro surfer, Kelly, who changes his life.

This is one of those books where I was able to combine my love for many things—tropical locales, surfing and hot marines! I hope you enjoy this fantasy trip to Fiji with Rafe and Kelly.

Also I hope you'll take a moment this month to remember all of our military heroes and heroines at home and overseas.

Enjoy!

Candace Havens

Mission: Seduction

—

Candace Havens

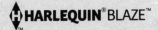

Recycling programs
for this product may
not exist in your area.

ISBN-13: 978-0-373-79768-4

MISSION: SEDUCTION

HARLEQUIN®

www.Harlequin.com

Printed in U.S.A.

ABOUT THE AUTHOR

Award-winning author and columnist Candace "Candy" Havens lives in Texas with her mostly understanding husband, two children and two dogs. Candy is a nationally syndicated entertainment columnist for FYI Television. She has interviewed just about everyone in Hollywood, from George Clooney and Orlando Bloom to Nicole Kidman and Kate Beckinsale. You can hear Candy weekly on The Big 96.3 in the Dallas–Fort Worth Area. Her popular online writer's workshop has more than 1,300 students and provides free classes to professional and aspiring writers.

Books by Candace Havens

HARLEQUIN BLAZE
523—TAKE ME IF YOU DARE
607—SHE WHO DARES, WINS
613—TRUTH *AND* DARE
646—MODEL MARINE

To get the inside scoop on Harlequin Blaze and its talented writers, be sure to check out blazeauthors.com.

Other titles by this author available in ebook format.
Don't miss any of our special offers. Write to us at the following address for information on our newest releases.

Harlequin Reader Service
U.S.: 3010 Walden Ave., P.O. Box 1325, Buffalo, NY 14269
Canadian: P.O. Box 609, Fort Erie, Ont. L2A 5X3

For Kathryn Lye.
For putting up with my kind of crazy!

1

THE BULLET ZINGED past marine lieutenant Rafe McCawley's ear. Instantly, he went into defense mode. "Jeep!" he yelled to the doctor and the ambassador as he shoved them toward the vehicle.

"Sniper," he told his men, but he knew they were already on it. As part of the rescue mission, they'd been trained for moments like this.

Buck and Meyers fired toward the hills.

Murphy had the car door open and helped the civilians in as fast as he could. Rafe used himself as a human shield.

Fire tore into his hip. He'd been hit.

He didn't falter.

He was the only thing between the sniper and the civilians, and it was his duty.

Pain scorched his right arm. Another bullet. He was a sitting duck, but it didn't matter. He had to get these people to safety.

Everything seemed to happen in slow motion then. A series of bullets pounded his back. His vest kept them from penetrating. The force knocked the breath from his lungs. He lunged forward in a final effort to protect the ambassador, half throwing the man into the vehicle so that Murphy could shut the door. As he did, blood stained Murphy's neck.

Rafe placed his hand at the wound to stop the blood flow, but he was losing blood, too, and he could feel himself getting weaker.

"Man down. Man down," Rafe heard himself utter as he slid into the darkness.

"Mister! Hey, mister! Wake up. Bad dreams, man. Bad dreams."

A groggy Rafe tried to open his eyes. It was as if someone had pulled him up out of quicksand.

"Mister, you okay? Wake up already."

Blinking his eyes open, Rafe took in his surroundings. A taxi. The driver, who had deeply tanned skin and a thatch of bright white hair, stared worriedly at him in the rearview mirror.

Rafe was in Fiji. Safe.

"Thanks," Rafe said to the driver. "Sorry for falling asleep." He must have passed out in the cab. The flight to Fiji had been brutal on his still-healing body, and he hadn't gotten much rest. Rafe scrubbed his face with his hand.

He was finally here.

Sun. Sea. And a woman.

Rafe figured that was all any man ever needed to heal wounds of the physical or mental variety. While he'd been in recovery for the injuries he'd suffered he'd thought of little else. The letters from Mimi were what kept him going through the intense therapy. Her sweet encouragement and kind words were the elixir his soul used to heal. And were exactly what his mind needed to help forget. Now he would see her in the next ten minutes.

The long hours on the plane here had been torture. His hip, arm and shoulder, which had suffered the brunt of the bullets in the firefight, were still sore. Even with his pain meds he couldn't get comfortable on the plane. He'd been awake for almost forty-eight hours straight. But he hadn't grumbled or even worried about it. The only thing in his mind was the image of the gorgeous five-eleven dark-haired beauty he was about to see. It had been eighteen months. He'd kicked himself for not kissing her at the end of their one and only date.

They met at a New York fashion show where Rafe had been duped into modeling some jeans that put him in hot water with the Marines. But it had been worth it to meet Mimi. After the fashion show, she'd taken him to a party with a lot of famous people. At the end of the evening, he'd walked her to her apartment but refused to go up. He was a gentleman, which seemed to surprise her. They hugged, and he left. The next day she flew out of town for a gig in London, and he hadn't seen her since.

She began writing to him six months ago. That first letter from her was a surprise. He'd written to her six months prior to that and when she hadn't answered, he thought that despite a great night she had moved on. In her first letter she told him that she traveled so much his letter must have slipped through the cracks.

They wrote back and forth frequently. He tried to get her on Skype or the phone, but things never appeared to work for Mimi when it came to electronics. She said it was one of her many faults. A few days before he'd been shot, he'd received a letter from her saying that as soon as he was free they should meet at her sister's new yoga and surf camp in Fiji. The time he was ordered to take off for rehab gave him the perfect excuse to accept her offer.

"Almost there," the taxi driver said as he swerved to miss a cyclist. Rafe's shoulder hit the side of the car and he winced. He was beginning to wonder if he'd ever be back to 100 percent. Every day he worked his muscles hard to make sure they didn't atrophy, but nothing moved quite as well as it should. And yet he needed to be ready for anything if he were to return to active duty one day.

The farther they drove away from the airport, the greener and more lush the surroundings. The cab's open windows allowed the smell of exotic flowers to permeate the air. The car stopped in front of iron gates covered with vegetation.

This was it.

The past year had been hell, and Rafe had to admit hanging out in paradise for a few weeks didn't sound too bad. Sure beat the hospital and his last three tours.

The driver pushed a button on the console at the side of the gate and the gate swung open.

The what-ifs plagued him. What if Mimi didn't recognize him? What if she was merely doing this to be nice?

For months he'd imagined swinging her in his arms and kissing her senseless when he saw her again to make up for the lost opportunity on their date.

Play it cool. Get a read on the situation.

He took a deep breath, then another.

The taxi stopped on the circular driveway in front of the resort. Well, it was more like a mansion than a hotel. Mimi said that her sister had worked hard to make it feel like a home away from home.

He grinned. It wasn't like any home he'd ever lived in. Mimi promised this was a great place to relax and rejuvenate and that was exactly what he needed.

As he glanced up, he realized there were several thatched dwellings along the beach on both sides of the house. They were probably the private bungalows Mimi mentioned. She was setting him up in one, all expenses paid.

He'd been hesitant about that, but she'd insisted, relaying to him that her sister had given her a great discount, since it was for a friend.

Grateful to stretch his legs again, he stepped out of the cab and was assaulted by the salty air coming off the sea. Surrounded by brilliant green foliage, it looked and sounded like a jungle. Birds chirped and there was even a monkey swinging in a nearby tree.

Yes, this was total bliss.

"Rafe?"

He turned and was expecting to see Mimi, but this woman didn't look anything like her. She was about the same height, but her hair was long and blond. And Mimi had looked as if she'd never been in the sun, whereas this woman was the color of golden honey.

She had a California girl-next-door quality that would normally be very appealing to him, but he was here to see Mimi.

He cleared his throat. "Yes, I'm Rafe. Are you a friend of Mimi's?"

She frowned and looked down at her toes for a second before glancing at him. "I'm her sister, Kelly. She's actually been delayed a few days. She had a shoot in

Canada of all places, and she asked me to look after you."

Rafe's heart sank. He knew it was silly to be so disappointed, but he'd been looking forward to seeing her.

"Oh. Hi." He wasn't sure what to say to this woman. "Uh...should I find someplace else to stay until she gets here?" He could probably find another hotel on the island. His friends told him the lodging and food in Fiji was usually pretty cheap, except at some of the larger, fancier hotels.

"No, no. How can I look after you if you stay somewhere else? No, I have you set up in the Blue Bungalow. Everything is done by color here. Your surfboard is blue, the instructions and times for your classes are in blue. Even the room is decorated in blue."

She paused and then gave him a worried glance. "You don't mind the color blue, do you?"

He chuckled. "No. It happens to be my favorite color, but I don't want to put you to any trouble. And what do you mean by classes?"

The taxi driver cleared his throat, and Rafe pulled out his wallet. "Sorry, man. Here you go." He gave the driver the money for the fare plus a generous tip. Then he picked up his pack and followed Kelly down a path.

"You asked about the classes," she said as they tracked along another path, clearly leading to the bungalows on the beach. "There are yoga and surfing classes. I also have Pilates, ballet bar, regular and Bikram yoga classes. They're popular with our usual clientele here at Last Resort."

From the looks of the surroundings that usual clientele must be pretty high-end. While it had a wild feel to it, the bungalows and the mansion or main building, which had to be at least ten thousand square feet, were very well maintained.

"I don't do any of those things," he said.

"I kn— Uh, right. Mimi said that she didn't think you'd go for it, but I also know that you are getting over some injuries. Surfing might be a little rough on you right now, but yoga could do you some good. And Pilates would help lengthen those muscles and relieve your pain."

He felt like a jerk for being so blunt. "You know what, I'm here. I might as well try whatever you have."

Turning, she smiled at him, her blue eyes shining with happiness.

Rafe's breath caught, and his lower regions responded so strongly he had to position his pack in front of him.

What is wrong with me?

She's a beautiful woman, but you are dating her sister.

Well, technically they weren't dating. But he'd flown halfway around the world to see her and that counted for something.

"I'm glad that you're so open-minded. I find that most women who come here are ready to try new things, but a lot of men are sometimes worried about looking ridiculous. And that's kind of ridiculous when you think about it. Tons of athletes from football players to track stars do yoga and Pilates. It's great for stress relief and it helps to clear your mind. We had a hockey team here about a month after I took over. Those guys were up for anything." Laughter colored her voice.

Clearing the mind was something Rafe needed desperately. The more Kelly talked, the more entranced he became with her. She was like a beacon of light and he was the ship in need of safe harbor. He snorted.

What you need is some sleep.

That was it. He was punch-drunk and slightly delirious. With his defenses down, he didn't have a chance when it came to Kelly, with her charm and beauty.

"So here we are." She waved a hand at the bungalow before him. The doors stood wide open, allowing the breeze to cool the large room, which was done in shades of light blue and white. Calming. It was nicer than any place he'd ever stayed. As a marine, he learned to fall asleep anywhere, and when he traveled he usually picked cheap motels. All he usually needed was a bed.

"Are you sure you don't mind me staying here?" Rafe asked as he ditched his shoes at the door and followed her inside.

The floor was cork or close enough by the soft feel of it. His aching joints relaxed their protest three steps into the place. There was a king-size bed on the left. To the right was a seating area with a huge flat-screen TV on the wall in the center, which could be viewed from both the bed and the sofa.

"Of course I don't mind. I wanted you to come, when, uh, Mimi told me what you'd been through. I mean, not to make a big deal out of it—your bravery— well, you're so darn heroic," she said, and ducked her head as if she were embarrassed. "Sorry. It's just that Mimi has told me so much about you that I feel like I know you. I'm normally kind of shy, which is why it's weird that I can't seem to stop talking around you."

She grinned sheepishly. "I'm going to stop talking now."

Rafe couldn't help but smile at her nervousness.

"Hey, you don't have to worry about that with me. I spend most of my time with men who only communicate by grunting. It's nice to hear a friendly voice that isn't barking orders."

Her soft chuckle was like a gentle caress. They stared at each other expectantly for a few seconds before he quickly peered at the ocean as though he was interested in the view.

"I bet you're exhausted," she said. "The bath is through there. There are robes and a selection of swim trunks if you need them. Dinner is at seven, but there are snacks in your fridge, which is under the television console. You have a butler, whom you can contact by pressing two on the phone. If you need maid service, that's number three. If you'd rather dine here instead of at the main house, you push four and they'll deliver the meal for you.

"So, that should be it. If you need me, push six and then seven, seven. We have several guests arriving, but practically everyone who comes to Last Resort is looking for solitude and waves to ride. It'll be quiet around here for you."

"Thanks," Rafe said. "I mean, really. This is way more than I expected."

The hopeful look in her eyes confused him. It was almost as if she'd worried he wouldn't like it here. How could he not? The place was mind-blowing.

"Right. If you need help unpacking, you can call the butler. I'll get out of your hair."

She sprinted from the bungalow.

He watched as she tripped slightly on the path and then carried on as if nothing had happened.

The two sisters couldn't be any more different. Mimi

never had a hair out of place, and the night they went to the party she had dressed in pricey heels and a fancy dress that barely covered her thighs.

But if he were honest, he much preferred Kelly's casual white shorts and bikini top.

"You aren't going there," he murmured to himself. "Mimi. You're here for Mimi."

Right. What's it to be, then—a cold shower or a nap? Nah.

Rafe glanced at the ocean and went in search of his board shorts.

A good hard swim would help ease his tension and get his mind off one very pretty resort owner.

2

"WHAT HAVE I done?" Kelly Callahan paced from one end of the kitchen to the other. Adrien, the resort's main chef, didn't bother to answer her. Though born in France, he'd grown up not far from where she had started surfing in Southern California. Still, half the time, he pretended he didn't understand her. Mimi, her sister, called him "tall, dark and dangerous," but to Kelly he was only ever one of her surfing buddies.

Kelly continued her rambling. "He's so much more hot in person. I mean, almost godlike. But there's such sadness in those beautiful eyes. The kind so deep you think it's never going to go away. If he finds out the truth—"

The third time she bumped into the chef, he shooed her out of his way by silently threatening her with a large spoon. She resumed pacing on the other side of the enormous breakfast bar they used to lay out a spread of fruits and pastries for guests to snack on throughout the day.

She picked up a muffin but didn't take a bite.

"No." She shook her head. "I should walk over there

right now and tell him everything. Rafe deserves to know."

Adrien mumbled something in French and waved his spoon again.

She stopped pacing long enough to lean forward to taste his soup. Closing her eyes, she savored the broth's spicy flavors against her tongue. Adrien never made a mistake with a meal.

"Why do you always have to do everything so well? Men! I swear. You're all so—argh."

Adrien's eyebrow lifted.

She squinted at him and stuck out her tongue.

He smiled triumphantly and went back to his soup.

During her rant, she'd accidentally smashed the uneaten muffin onto the counter. She felt guilty about that, too. She hated to waste food.

Nearby, she could hear some guests returning from a catamaran outing. Time for Kelly to get a hold of herself. It wouldn't do for the guests to see her in the middle of a nervous breakdown.

After dumping the muffin in the trash, she went to her suite to wash her hands. Her rooms were the only private bedroom and sitting room on the first floor and possessed the best sea views. Outfitted in colors of soft ivory and chocolate-brown, her suite could have been in any exclusive hotel in the world. She'd been lucky. When she bought Last Resort, it had been made over only a few months before. However, a high-end destination like this needed constant maintenance. There was always something that needed to be fixed, replaced or updated. The staff, most of whom she'd inherited with the buy, kept the place running smoothly. Some of them had been doing the same jobs since before she was born, so she left them to it.

After washing her hands, she sat down on the edge of her bed. Staring at her cell phone, she contemplated her next move. Mimi had to be told. Maybe she could convince her sister to temporarily go along with the ruse until Rafe was feeling better. She remembered the way his face fell when he found out Mimi wasn't there. Kelly winced. There was no way Rafe would be interested in her if Mimi was around.

She lay back on the bed. "It's not supposed to be about that," she chastised herself. "It's about helping him to get better."

Initially, when Kelly had invited Rafe, her sole intention had been to help him. He never whined or complained, but she could always tell that he had seen things he'd rather forget. After several letters prodding him about his injuries, he'd finally told her everything. That he'd nearly died sent her heart reeling. That was when she knew she cared much more than she should.

In her mind and in her heart, she knew she could make a positive difference in his life.

She turned onto her side.

Rafe was even more than she had expected. His inner strength only intensified his attractiveness. She thought of his taut muscles and the way his jeans fit against his—

"Stop it," she moaned. Even before she'd seen him, he had been a late-night fantasy. He'd often kept her awake as she wondered what it would be like if he touched her. Or better yet, kissed her.

Kelly quickly got out her cell phone and called her

sister. She had to tell someone the truth, or she would die from guilt.

"This is Mimi, you know what to do," the recorded voice said.

For a second Kelly thought about leaving the whole twisted story in a message. It would be so much easier, but she wouldn't stoop that low.

"Call me," she said before hitting the end call button.

"I'm not a bad person," she whispered to her pillows. "This all began so innocently. Can I help it if his letters made me fall for him? Is it my fault that I want him all to myself?"

A little voice in the back of her mind spoke up. "Oh, be quiet, conscience."

She needed something to do so she would stop obsessing. There was always paperwork, but she couldn't concentrate.

Jumping up from the bed, she slipped off her shorts, revealing the rest of her bikini. She then reached for the latch and opened the sliding glass door.

Outside, her board stood waiting for her. She grabbed it and ran to do the one thing that always soothed her.

It only took a moment for her feet to hit the warm sand. Curling her toes, she watched as the waves broke over the sandbar. The motion of the water was the balm she needed.

Running, she dove with her board into the first wave. *Home.*

RAFE STARED AS Kelly surfed one wave after another. The way she maneuvered the surfboard with such ease made him curious as to how someone so slim could tame the churning ocean. At first, he thought she must have to really focus on what she was doing, but she did it all so smoothly and controlled, she was clearly a natural.

When she hit the beach, she frowned and headed again into the surf.

Rafe didn't know her, but he did know human nature and she was worried about something.

That bothered him. She was such a kind soul. He'd recognized that about her from the instant they'd met. That and the fact that she'd welcomed him to her resort without a second thought. There was an immediate connection between them, one that disturbed Rafe because of its strength. The pull toward her was something that should only come after knowing a person for months, not minutes.

What amazed him the most was how fast he was over his initial disappointment of Mimi not being there to greet him.

Stop it.

He kicked his feet and swam back to shore. Once there, he claimed the towel he'd brought with him and sat down on the sand.

Had she felt the same awareness? Just because Kelly had been nice to him was no reason for him to think she might be interested in him.

Give it up.

You're here to hang out with her sister.

"Those look like some deep thoughts," Kelly said. She stood before him with her board stuck in the sand. How had she snuck up on him like that?

Great, marine, just great.

"Not so deep, I promise. You're a great surfer. I mean, I don't know much about the sport, but you ride those man-crushing waves like a pro." Rafe had stayed in shallow water to avoid the large swells, which rolled in higher by the minute.

"I am," she said.

He gave her a questioning look.

"A pro," she said, and laughed. "I surf professionally on the circuit. At least, I did until a few months ago before I decided to hit Pause for a bit and buy this place." She nodded toward the resort.

If she made enough to afford this luxury spot, she had to have done pretty well as an athlete.

Rafe chastised himself for staring at her. Bikini bottoms with tiny red bows at the hips flattered her long, tanned legs. Her flat stomach was slightly ripped with muscles, just enough to show she wasn't afraid of a good workout.

Rafe cleared his throat as he stood up. The interest in her toned-in-every-way body had to stop. He searched his brain to recall what they'd been talking about. "Why did you hit Pause?"

She pursed her lips. "Maybe that's the wrong expression. I think of it as a long vacation. To reevaluate what I want to do next with my life." She shifted from one foot to the other. "I've been traveling the world from one competition to the next since I was sixteen. Burnouts happen a lot in my sport. And to be honest, I was heading that way. I forgot my love for surfing and I wanted to remember why I'm addicted to those waves. And it's helped. A month's gone by and I'm already anticipating the next big meet.

"Listen to me. I sound like some confused chick trying to find herself."

"No, you don't," Rafe said quickly. "I love being an

active marine and serving, but there are some days I want to give it all a rest and be a farmer or something."

She grinned. Her amusement pleased him. "You don't seem like the farmer type."

"That *would* be kind of funny, since I don't know a thing about it," he admitted. "But some job where you work with your hands and you're alone out in nature. There's no one to report to, and you don't have to constantly watch your back."

That was true. After his last assignment, he'd begun to reevaluate what was important to him. Unlike Kelly, he had no idea what might be next. He had invested in his friend Will's private security company so he would always have a job there. That was his safety net.

But Rafe seldom took the safe path. His beat-up leg and shoulder were proof of that.

"How did you end up here? Seems like a lot to take on for one person."

She shrugged. "I'd been coming here for years during my off time because the waves are great for most of the year. A friend of mine owned it. One day he said he wanted to sell it, and everything fell into place so easily that I knew it was the right decision. It is a lot of work, but manageable. For the most part, it can run itself as long as there's someone to oversee the accounting and business stuff. Everyone who works here has been here for years, so that also helps."

Rafe studied her. Kelly was proud of what she'd accomplished, and she should be. From what he'd seen so far, this was about as close to paradise as one could get.

"So what time did you say dinner was?"

"Oh, thanks for the reminder. I need to get back there. It's at seven, and it's casual. Very casual. Shorts are fine. Well, see ya tonight." She grabbed her board and swung away with a jaunty lift to her step.

Rafe couldn't take his eyes off her bikini-clad body striding up the beach. The woman was insanely beautiful. It wasn't fair.

He laughed.

What was paradise without a little temptation?

3

RAFE SPOTTED KELLY from the open glass doors of his cabana. She was dressed in a white T-shirt and dark shorts. A pair of pink flip-flops graced her feet.

Yep. She was as hot as he remembered.

Hell.

What was he going to do? Rafe lived by the code of the corps, but he had his own code, as well. Before he'd ever thought about the Marines, his mother had instilled in him a profound respect for women. His father was strict when it came to treating others as equals. Rafe had grown up in the melting pot that was New York, and on his block everyone knew everyone else's business. There was no chance of getting away with treating a girl he dated any less than was expected.

Kelly leaned over to hand someone a drink, and he couldn't avoid it—the way her shorts stretched over her butt nearly sent him back to the showers for a cold one. As he approached the group of other guests, he noticed the man she'd given the drink to follow her with his eyes. The appreciation on his face didn't sit well with Rafe.

Hey, weren't you doing the same thing?
Shut up.

There were several people gathered in the mansion's central room. A big flat-screen was on in one corner where some of the men watched a soccer match. An older couple admired the fish in the aquarium that separated the room from the dining area. Rafe wondered how they kept the tank clean. It was enormous.

"Rafe, I'm so glad you're here," Kelly said as if she were surprised to see him.

The confusion must have shown on his face.

"After so many hours on the plane and the swim you took earlier, I thought maybe jet lag might have taken over."

He returned her smile. "It did—I passed out for a while, which is why I'm late. Sorry about that." In truth, it had taken everything he had to push himself out of bed and into the shower. Only the curiosity of wanting to see Kelly again had kept him going.

Careful there.

"Can I get you a drink?" she asked.

Rafe shook his head. He'd taken two pain pills so that he could make the walk over, and the doctors had warned him not to mix them with liquor.

"Nah, I'm good. Maybe some water?"

"Kelly, the dinner is ready," announced a lithe teen with the same beautiful skin of the Fijians and bright blue eyes that spoke of another ancestry.

"Are you sure you want to do this?" Kelly asked the young girl.

She nodded.

"Okay, but if you spill anything—"

"I know, I know." The girl almost rolled her eyes but stopped. "Sorry. Yes, ma'am."

The girl left them, presumably for the kitchen.

"Nari reminds me of myself," Kelly said softly. "I would do anything to surf when I was a kid."

"I don't follow," Rafe said.

"Oh, she helps out around the resort and occasionally waits tables to pay for her surf lessons here."

"You give lessons?"

"That she does, mate," said the man who had been watching Kelly when Rafe had shown up. The Australian was nearly as tall as Rafe's six-foot-four, but he had white-blond hair and the body of a boxer. Big biceps, short neck. Rafe couldn't imagine the guy on a surfboard.

"This is Josh," Kelly said as she introduced them.

"Rafe," he said as he stuck out his hand.

"Ah. You're the soldier Kelly was telling the Seymours about. Been in Afghanistan, I heard, and you were shot up pretty bad."

Rafe glanced at her to find her cheeks were pink.

"Gracie is a doctor," Kelly said. "I…had heard about how you'd been wounded and I wanted to make sure we had the right therapies for you, and that we didn't push you too hard. I promise we weren't gossiping."

"You don't need to worry about me," Rafe said. "As long as there's a gym, I can follow up with what my trainers started in Germany."

"Best facility on the island," Josh told him, and slapped him on the shoulder in a friendly gesture. Rafe struggled not to wince as a shot of pain raced down his back and into his aching hip. He reminded himself he was lucky to be alive. Unfortunately, there were few places on his body that hadn't felt the effect of his time in the military.

"Yep, they'll get you fixed up, all right. Came here a couple weeks ago to recover from a bruised hamstring and lower back troubles, and boom!" The man clapped his hands together eliciting a few startled glances. "All better now. This little chicken knows what she's up to. Got me back to fighting form months before the docs thought it would be possible," Josh announced to the group, squeezing Kelly into the crook of his arm.

Rafe took pleasure in the fact that she didn't seem too happy about being smashed up against the guy.

"Josh, can you check that the doors to the kitchen are closed? I want to make sure we don't get sand in there and it looks like the wind is picking up."

"On it." The Aussie lumbered through the main room over to the dining area.

"Are you okay?" Kelly asked softly. The light caress of her hand on Rafe's forearm was enough to send him over the edge. "He has no idea how strong he is."

"No worries," Rafe told her, his voice deeper than usual because her hand was still gently stroking his arm. "Do you always order your guests around like that?"

It was a subtle way to find out if she and the Australian were close.

"Yes," she replied with a laugh. "I'm bossy that way. Just ask my sister."

At the mention of her sister, she lifted her hand from his arm and frowned. "Sorry. What were we talking about before that?"

"About you being bossy," he said as he studied her carefully. Was there something bothering her about Mimi?

"Oh, yes. And with Josh, well, he was supposed to

be here for a week and it's turned into several. That happens a lot. Almost everyone who visits says they feel like family, so I guess it doesn't hurt to treat them that way. We have a fairly exclusive clientele who are used to plenty of perks, but they like it here because they get all that and they get to be surf bums at the same time. There's no paparazzi or helicopters flying over to see what kind of bikini they're wearing or what they're drinking, or who they are with for that matter." She shrugged.

"I thought I recognized some faces on the beach today."

She nodded. "Yeah, I'm sure you did. They keep coming back, since no one bugs them here. It's always been my sanctuary when life got to be too much on the circuit, and I wanted to create that for other people as well."

Sanctuary. If it weren't for his dilemma with the sisters, this place would definitely be that. The waves had put him to sleep in seconds after his head hit the pillow. The bungalow was warm, but the sea breeze kept it from being miserably so.

Rafe wasn't overly impressed with the boxer, but he understood why he was drawn to the place. It was the kind of environment a person could get used to easily. As Rafe sat down at the table across from Kelly, she gave him another smile.

Yep. He could definitely see why people never wanted to leave.

KELLY CROSSED HER legs on the special platform Nari's father, Duke, had made for her.

Meditation was part of Kelly's regular routine and,

no matter what was happening around her, she did it twice a day. Settling on the raised part of the deck outside her bedroom, she took a deep, calming breath and tried to clear her mind.

Adrien would kill her for not finishing her dinner tonight, but Kelly's nerves were like taut guitar strings ready to break. She'd have to speak to Josh about his being a little too handsy. Every chance he had, he put his arm around her shoulders or bent into her as if they were sharing a secret. He'd been overly friendly before, but Rafe's presence must have caused him to turn territorial. She and Josh had known each other a long time, but that didn't mean he could take advantage of their friendship.

His behavior probably gave Rafe the idea that they might be a couple, which was the last thing she wanted. She'd caught Rafe's eyes on them more than once during the meal and he had the strangest look on his face. She was adept at reading people, but she didn't have a clue what was happening in the marine's head. He'd been polite throughout dinner even though she'd seen him wince more than once when he twisted the wrong way.

He'd caught the soup tureen when it slipped from Nari's hands, keeping it from crashing to the floor. But his jaw had tightened and his hand shook as he placed the heavy bowl on the table.

In spite of his pain, he'd assured the young girl that all was well. His kindness toward the fumbling Nari had solidified his hold on Kelly's heart. And, as if that wasn't enough, she'd admitted she was infatuated with him before he'd even arrived.

What had begun as an act of kindness on her part for one of America's heroes had now morphed into a complicated situation that confused her. What should she do? He was an honorable man who appreciated the truth. After seeing that up close and personal, she felt certain he would leave if he knew she'd lied to get him here.

She truly cared about him. And if he left before he really got to know who she was, she'd regret it for the rest of her life. Maybe he would, too.

Helping him heal was the one way she could clear her conscience and set her karma straight. He'd been through so much, the least she could do was support him as he tried to put the pieces of his life back together again. She'd recognized the signs of post-traumatic stress syndrome in his letters. His trouble sleeping, the nightmares, his erratic moods. He'd shared a lot with her, and now she knew what she had to do to repay that trust.

Taking another calming breath, she shut her eyes, but just before her mind went blank, a vision of Rafe on the beach overtook her thoughts. Water dripped from his dark hair, his swim trunks riding low on his hips, his chiseled jaw and toned abs some of the best she'd ever seen on a man.

She sighed.

Well, no one ever said karmic justice was easy.

4

RAFE LIMPED INTO the yoga studio, ready to tell Kelly he wasn't up for her class. Like the cabana where he was staying, the studio and adjoining gym had glass sliding doors so that the view was of sand and ocean.

Before he could apologize for backing out of the class, the sight before him rocked him to the core.

Kelly, pawing through yoga mats, was dressed in pink shorts and a skin-tight bra top. He thanked the heavens for blessing him with this particular moment in time.

Rafe wasn't sure if he should continue to ogle or announce himself, but she peeked up at him.

"Hey," she said. "I'm trying to find you a mat. We have larger ones for tall people, but they're in the bottom of the box."

At the mention of *bottom,* he turned around to leave, but the Seymours were just arriving. Gracie was a physical therapist and her brother a trainer for a college football team. They were friends of Kelly's who worked the pro-surfing circuit while putting themselves through college. Behind them was James Limon, one of the most popular directors in Hollywood. He and Rafe had discussed Limon's time serving in the Gulf War and about his passion for surfing. He'd encouraged Rafe to try the sport when he was feeling up to it.

With nowhere left to hide his appreciation of Kelly, he rushed over to the box and knelt, as best he could, next to her.

"Here," he said, grabbing onto the first mat he spotted. Thankfully, she couldn't see the evidence her fine body had on his body. When he lifted his head, his eyes were level with her breasts.

Rafe sucked in a breath. He'd survived three tours, and now the universe was determined to kill him with her beauty.

"Oh, are you okay?" She was stared at him worriedly. "You shouldn't kneel with your leg the way it is. Let me help you up."

Panicked, Rafe mumbled, "I'm fine," and made his way to the back of the class. Others had joined in while he'd been talking to Kelly.

By the time she began the class, there were four women and three men, one of whom looked like a pro baseball player, but Rafe wasn't sure. Everyone put their mats on the floor and rolled them out. He couldn't quite do that yet.

Facing the back wall, he willed his body to calm down. He forced himself to think of the last time that he'd been shot. The muscles in his body clenched, but the pain solved his problem. A few seconds later, he sat on the floor like the rest of the group.

Well, almost. His legs didn't quite cross the way theirs did. He put the pads of his feet together. That was as much as he could do with his stiff leg.

"This is rehab yoga," Kelly announced from the front of the class as she sat down and crossed her legs. "We have a new guest—Rafe."

Everyone turned to smile and wave at him. He gave them a grin that was probably a bit more like a grimace, as his sore leg chose that moment to tense up in a charley horse.

His jaw tightened as he worked the muscle with the heel of his hand and then flexed his foot so the calf could lengthen.

"These exercises are done on the floor to ease the muscular pressure one might experience if doing them in a regular yoga class," Kelly explained. "Today is about stretching and helping those muscles to relax so your body can heal. Okay, let's start in the lotus position. That's good, Rafe. If you need to you can separate the soles of your feet," Kelly instructed. "You should not feel pain."

Rafe's groin wasn't happy about where his legs needed to go, but he ignored the pain. He didn't have the heart to tell Kelly that the pain never left his body. It served as a constant reminder that he was human and just as mortal as the next guy.

In the military, he'd been taught that he could do anything. Survive anything. But as they moved through the next two positions, he wondered if his body would ever recover from Kelly's pretzel-like torture.

No pain, my ass.

"Now lift your arms up and over your head as we open ourselves to the sun."

As she gracefully extended her arms above her head, Rafe noticed her top pulled tightly against her chest. He'd never make it through the class if he didn't stop looking at her. Leaving was his best option, but he didn't want to disappoint her. She had such high hopes that her classes would be beneficial for him.

Doing his best to stop staring at her, he switched his attention to the other men in the class and followed their actions. Finally, Rafe brought himself and his rebellious libido under control.

Until he glanced over and saw Kelly with her legs stretched wide.

As the class neared its end, Rafe's muscles relaxed for the first time in months. Amazingly, the exercises had helped his leg. His muscles seemed considerably looser. The group was attempting one last stretch when Kelly put her hand on his ankle to turn his foot the right way.

"You want to keep it perpendicular so that you don't pull on those hip tendons too much." She gave him one of her dazzling smiles, and he was lost. Her gentle touch sent heat through his body.

"Thanks," he said roughly, using every bit of his control to keep himself in check.

Her eyes narrowed slightly as if she were trying to figure something out, but she returned to the front of the class to do the last bit where they lay down on the mat to rest.

Rafe now equated yoga to sexual gymnastics. Sure it worked, but he was exhausted. A shower and a nap were next on his agenda.

"Close your eyes, and listen to the waves," her gentle voice directed. "Feel the movement of the water as it caresses your body and sends you to your happy place… that Zen only you can find.

"Namaste."

The sound of the waves filled Rafe's head, and his body became so light that it seemed to float out over the ocean. He hadn't been this calm in years.

"Rafe?" Kelly's voice penetrated his thoughts. "Are you okay?"

He didn't want anyone interrupting this peaceful feeling. Gesturing toward her, he hoped she'd get the message.

Kelly giggled, and his eyes popped open. She was biting her lip to keep from laughing.

"What's so funny?" he asked.

"You," she replied sweetly. "I bet you were riding those waves like a Zen pro."

Rafe chuckled. "I don't know about that, but I have to stop making fun of froufrou yoga crap. I feel better than I have in months, maybe years. You're a great teacher."

"Thanks." She extended a hand to help him up.

Rafe was shocked to find they were the only ones in the studio. "Where did everyone go?"

"You've been like that for about fifteen minutes. I let you rest while I cleaned up. I would have just left you there, but I worried your hip might stiffen on the hard floor."

"Right. Well, I guess I'd better hit the shower. We didn't move that much, although I did sweat."

"Yes, it's funny what happens when you are really working those muscles. Why don't you take your shower, and I'll put you down for a massage later this afternoon. Mason, one of our top masseurs, has terrific hands, and it will be good to get in there and work those muscles while they're relaxed."

"Great idea. See you later," he said as he rushed out. The woman affected him like no other.

Walking straight into the ocean, Rafe used the cold water to rein in his libido again. This might be the longest two weeks of his life if he didn't find a way to manage his attraction to Mimi's sister.

RAFE WANTED HER. Kelly put her hand over her heart. The very impressive bulge in those loose shorts was impossible to miss.

She stared after him while he all but ran into the waves. His broad back, muscular shoulders and that tattoo of the rising phoenix across his back didn't help the runaway train her emotions had become. The man was too hot for words.

Was that really in response to her? He'd avoided eye contact with her for most of the class and watched Clifton during the exercises instead. At first, she thought it was because he wanted to see the male version of the moves, but now she wasn't so sure. Did she have that kind of sexual sway over him? She had to know.

"Rafe," she called as she jogged out onto the beach.

"Yes?" He didn't turn around.

"Your massage appointment is set for noon, and I've ordered some special oils that soothe aches and pains."

"Okay." His voice sounded strained.

She cleared her throat, stifling the urge to smile. Yes, she definitely had an effect on him.

Last night, she'd promised herself she would be a good friend to the marine and get him back into tip-top shape.

But knowing he wanted her as much as she did him— at least she hoped—changed the game entirely.

An hour later, Rafe showed up at the spa wearing a crisp white T-shirt and royal-blue board shorts.

The man could have been a model the way he wore clothes.

Kelly ushered him into one of the Zen rooms, as they called them. She lit a candle and switched on some soothing music.

"Strip down, okay? That way the therapist can work on your hip."

"Got it," he said.

"We always ask if you would like a silent massage. Some people like to have only music without any talking so they can relax. Other people need the chatter because they may not be comfortable with someone touching them so—*intimately.* The choice is yours."

He nodded. "I like the idea of the quiet one," he said, his face a mask.

Oh, yes, this would work out perfectly.

"Excellent, so the masseur will be in shortly. When you are undressed and on the table facedown, you can push the button to the right." She pointed to a small panel next to the massage table.

Then she left.

While he stripped, she changed into a white T-shirt, which she knotted under her breasts, and a pair of short gray workout shorts.

Once the light flipped on above the door, she entered.

Rafe was facedown on the table, a sheet covering his lower half.

Coating her hands in oil and eucalyptus, Kelly smoothed one hand down his back. Two small scars peppered his shoulder and there were three more on the right hip.

Poor Rafe. Most people had no idea how much these guys suffered for their country. Heart swelling with pride, it was all she could do not to lean down and kiss each scar. She moved on to his shoulders, his body relaxed and his breathing slowed. Her fingers dug into the tendons between his neck and right shoulder and she heard him groan slightly as the tension gave way.

When she reached his scalp, he let out a deep breath.

Kelly grinned. That she could bring him such relief was a balm for her soul. Massaging his temples, she felt him jerk suddenly.

"Kelly," his deep voice rasped.

How had he known it was her?

"Is something wrong?" she asked lightly. "Is the pressure too much?"

"No, I was—uh—just surprised that you were the one doing the massage. I thought you said someone named Mason was doing it."

"His current client requested an extra thirty minutes. Would you rather have a male? I'm sorry. I would've asked if I thought it would be a problem."

Liar.

"No. That's fine." Rafe coughed. "Could I have some water?"

"Sure," she said as she wiped her hands on a towel. She handed him a bottle of water she'd brought in just in case he needed it.

He lifted his head so that he could drink, and his gaze met her face.

"Hi," he said. That one word was filled with so much desire that she felt it in her bones.

"Hi," she said back. "In case you're wondering about the massage, I am licensed. All the surfers on my pro team are trained so that we can help each other during competitions if we get beat up a little. Competition sites don't always have chiropractors or massage therapists available."

He took a long drink and then handed the bottle of water back to her.

"I believe you," he said before putting his face back into the horseshoe-shaped hole at the top of the table. "If you don't mind, maybe we could just focus on my back and legs for now."

"Rafe, if you're worried about tents rising in the middle of the massage, don't." She couldn't believe she'd just said that out loud. "Massage is a sensual experience. If it makes you feel any better, I can put extra towels over your pelvis, but I need to get deep down into those upper thigh and hip muscles if we want to do something about the source of your pain."

He didn't say anything.

"And for the record," she stated, in her best professional sounding voice, "that happens a lot with me. In fact, it's more unusual if it doesn't."

"You mean, almost every guy you massage gets, uh, aroused for you?" He didn't sound happy about that news.

"Not for me, silly. It's the body's natural response given the circumstances." She was being clinical, but when it came to Rafe, she was anything but. She couldn't wait to get her hands on his body.

"I don't like the idea of you working on guys like that. I mean, it doesn't seem safe. Some might try to take advantage of the situation and…"

Kelly gave an unladylike snort. "I don't do happy endings, Rafe. I'm a professional, but not that kind."

He sighed. "Sorry, I didn't mean to imply that you were. It's just that— Oh hell, I give up."

"Let's get you back into that relaxed state," she said as her hands slid down his back again. She liked that he was slightly possessive and didn't want her touching other men. Usually, she didn't go for that type of guy, but with Rafe it was damn sexy.

Relaxed? Not likely. Rafe squeezed his eyes shut.

Why did he feel so protective toward this woman? The idea that Kelly touched other men in this way—it turned his gut.

What is wrong with you?

And how many times had he asked himself that question since he'd arrived at Last Resort? He didn't want to admit it, but he knew *exactly* what was wrong with him. He had it bad for Mimi's sister—in the worst possible way. In fact, he had it in a way that he'd never had before. This innate interest in her and need to take care of her was something completely new to him.

Sweet and so gorgeous, Kelly took his breath away. He had never believed in the ideal woman. The sexy woman, the fun woman, the marrying woman, even the nurturing woman, but Kelly filled all those categories and more. When he'd opened his eyes and saw her bright pink toenail polish, he'd nearly jumped off the massage table.

Strong, smooth hands pummeled and pushed his body. His cock was so hard that it hurt. Slim fingers worked the muscles in his upper right thigh and hip.

"Wow, you have a lot of tension here," she said as she used her elbow to press effectively into his flesh.

No joke. If she could see his pelvis, she'd run for the

hills. Tent nothing—he had a battleship underneath, ready to go to war with those precious hands of hers.

"Time to turn over." She held up the sheet to give him some privacy. He couldn't do it.

Ripping the sheet from her hands, he tightened it around himself as he rolled awkwardly off the table. Scooping up his shorts with one hand, he ran for the door. It was a full-on strategic retreat. He was not here to seduce Mimi's sister. And yet, if he let her put her hands on him one more time, then that was exactly what would happen.

"Rafe?"

He couldn't look back.

"Uh, I think I left the coffeemaker on in my room," he said as he threw open the door.

Her soft, hesitant laugh caught him as he double-timed it out of the building.

She knew as well as he did that there were no coffeemakers in the rooms.

Standing under the cold spray of the shower in his room, Rafe tried to calm himself down, but it was impossible. He made the water warmer and grasped his cock.

Memories of Kelly flashed through his brain. Kelly on her surfboard, so free and happy. Kelly in her sexy pink yoga clothes. Kelly with that flat, tanned stomach under her knotted T-shirt. The woman was driving him mad with wanting her, and she was absolutely clueless.

When he started to imagine that sweet voice of hers begging him to make love to her, it was more than he could take. He came so hard he had to brace himself against the shower wall.

Gasping for breath, he let the water sluice down his

body, rinsing away his need for her. He had to do something about this before it got any worse.

Maybe I should find somewhere else to stay? After
all, what would she think of him if he dared to act on his
urges? He had gone there to spend time with her sister.

Rafe rejected the idea of leaving, though, the moment it occurred to him. No way, wasn't going to happen, he told himself. He didn't want to be away from
her. So even if he couldn't—or rather, shouldn't—have
her, he'd still spend as much time with her as possible.
She might drive his body wild, but she was a balm for
his soul. The previous night had been the first without nightmares in years. He'd been so consumed with
thoughts about her before he fell asleep that she'd filled
his dreams.

"Rafe?" Hell, she was in his room.

"In the shower," he called out to her. "Just a minute."

He doused himself in freezing cold water to dampen
the fire raging in his blood. Twisting off the knob, he
sucked in a breath and wrapped a towel around his
waist.

Just as he went from the bathroom into the bedroom,
Kelly was setting an envelope on his pillow.

"Oh." Her eyes flashed wide, and he watched as her
gaze traveled from his chest all the way down to his
toes and back up to his face. "I—"

Obviously, he affected her as much as she did him.
Grim satisfaction surged through him. Her demeanor
was exactly the sign Rafe needed—well, once he settled
matters with Mimi. And he couldn't rush at Kelly like
he wanted to. This would take time. She was special,
and he didn't want to screw it up by coming across like
some horny teenager.

"Sorry, I couldn't hear you," he told her, and gave her his best smile.

"That's—" she swallowed hard "—okay. I wanted to see if you'd be my date, well, not actually a date, maybe escort. No, no, that isn't right, either." She looked in one direction then another as if flustered.

"I'm happy to go wherever you need me to."

"I was hoping that it might be nice for you to meet some of the ex-pats who live here," she said. "What I was trying to say is that *we* could go together to this party that one of my sponsors is throwing tonight. I want to show my face so that they don't forget about me."

No one could ever forget her, of that he was certain.

He couldn't tell her no, and in fact, he didn't want to.

"What do I need to wear?"

"It's always casual around here. Jeans or shorts and a shirt would be great. It starts at eight, but we don't need to get there until about nine. That's when the band plays." She turned and all but bounced from the room.

Band, that meant the possibility of dancing. Rafe smiled slowly. He didn't mind that one bit. Even with his bum leg he might be able to do a slow dance or three.

Thoughts of holding her close appealed to him.

"And lunch is ready when you are," she announced, stopping at the doorway to face him. She was fiddling with her hair and at one point she slapped her hands together. The fidgeting was provocative and inviting. He wanted to catch her hands in his and pull her close to him right then.

Never in his life had he wanted a woman so much. It was the universe messing with his head. If he played the gentleman like he'd planned to, he might never taste her lips or—

No. That wasn't likely.

He kept his hands fisted at his sides and the towel in place. She gave him another one of those shy, sexy smiles and escaped into sand and sunshine.

Pressing flesh with Kelly was definitely intriguing, but he had a code he lived by. If he could possibly avoid it, he wouldn't hurt her or Mimi.

He needed a solution and fast.

Picking up his cell phone, Rafe prayed that he could reach Mimi in time.

5

THE CALIFORNIA TAN girls surrounded Rafe like an impenetrable wall of bikini-clad models. They were there to promote tanning lotion, but they seemed more interested in the marine. Kelly couldn't blame them. Given his rough good looks and firm body, he was like a god. Her palms itched to once again get her fingers on his rock-hard body. And those blue eyes…she could gaze into them all night. The man was absolutely breathtaking.

One of the brunettes pulled a small bottle of California Tan from between her breasts and rubbed the lotion into Rafe's hand as she gave him a sensual smile.

Rafe tried to pull away.

Kelly's mouth flattened into a straight line. Enough was enough. Rafe was hers. Well, technically he was her sister's, but she couldn't stand the thought of those women touching him.

They had to go.

Her plans to get rid of the annoying models conflicted, however, with the guilt nibbling at her conscience. Earlier, she'd listened to Rafe's voice mail message. Believing he was talking to Mimi, he'd told her that something crazy had happened. He'd called twice and after getting no answer, he said he needed to go ahead and set the record straight so he wasn't leading her on.

"You've been so kind to me the last few months," he'd said earnestly in his message. "But the truth is, I've found someone who— Well, I really want to see where it goes. The woman, that part I would like to talk to you about in person. It's complicated. I didn't want to do this over the phone, but I've never been able to get a hold of you. Thank you so much for sending me here to Fiji. It's turned out to be one of the most amazing trips of my life. I hope wherever you are that you're having a great time. And thank you again for keeping my spirits up while I was in the hospital. Bye."

Kelly had deleted the message and hugged herself. He was an honest and honorable man. She needed to be honest with him, too.

"We need to talk," said Greg, her manager, interrupting her thoughts.

She sighed. He wouldn't let up on her about returning to the circuit. She wasn't ready yet, but he didn't want to hear that.

"It's a party, Greg. I don't want to talk about business, and I haven't changed my mind."

He held up his hands in surrender. "I promise I won't nag, babe. Just want to share some good news."

Kelly narrowed her eyes at him. Greg wasn't a bad guy, but the only thing he cared about was the bottom line. Of course, she was the last one to complain about that since his concern for the bottom line was one of the many reasons she never had to worry about money.

She could live in paradise for the rest of her life if she wanted to. Still, even though she believed he had her best interests at heart, he didn't understand the emotional side of what she needed.

That was something they'd both learned when they dated a few years ago. They were friends as well as business partners and he'd seen her through the good and the bad times. Then one day she looked at him and saw someone other than "the boss," as she called him. She had the flu and he didn't want her on the water until she was better. But it was one of the biggest meets of the year, and she refused to miss it.

She'd won the event but couldn't even paddle in, she was so tired. He swam out to get her and carried her straight to the doctor's office.

At first, she and Greg seemed like the perfect match. She so appreciated everything he was doing for her career, until she realized that crossing their private and professional boundaries meant that he would act as if he owned her. She broke up with him when he started to agree to things on her behalf without checking with her first.

She should have fired him, but she was loyal to a fault.

He motioned to the tables on the terrace overlooking the sea. "Fine, let's talk." But she frowned as she noticed the cloying girls circling Rafe.

She followed Greg to a quiet spot, impatient to get this over with.

"So," Greg began, grinning as he set his beer glass in front of him. "Baywear wants you as a spokesmodel for their new clothing line and they are willing to pay big to make that happen."

Kelly bit her lip. She'd wanted to be a Baywear girl all of her life. One of her surfing mentors, Roz Mazur, had been one. It was a sign that you had made it to the top. A dream come true. "What's the catch?" she asked.

Greg shrugged. "There's travel involved. You'd have to do their larger events at different tournaments, print and online ads and commercials. The contract they're offering is for two million dollars, but you'll be on the road at least eighty days a year."

Kelly fidgeted in her chair. It made sense they'd want to get the most for their money. And eighty days was nothing compared to what she had done the past few years with more than two hundred days on the road.

"I'd have to find a full-time manager for the resort."

"Yeah, listen, about that. I have an excellent buyer for you. He's willing to pay three times what you did. Believe me, it's probably the best deal you'll ever get." The blasé delivery coupled with Greg's outright audacity delivered a one-two punch to her gut.

Glancing up at the sky, she fought to control her temper. "Why would you even mention selling *my* place? I told you I don't plan on ever selling it. What is wrong with you? You never listen to me. It's always about the money with you. I thought you cared about what's best for me, but it's obvious that you don't." Her raised voice was drawing the attention of the nearby crowd.

"What? I'm not supposed to tell you when some guy approaches me out of the blue and wants to buy your property? Whatever may have happened between us before, you're wrong, babe. I always want what's best for you." He shook his head. "You don't make it easy though. You could take that money and buy two more resorts, if you wanted."

She growled in frustration. He always had an answer for everything. And getting angry wouldn't work. He'd shut down and give her that patronizing look. The one that said he'd wait until she calmed down and became a reasonable human being.

She hated that look.

"I don't want three resorts. I only want Last Resort. What's wrong with that?"

His eyebrows shot up. "You'd walk away from a cash deal like this one for some big house by the beach."

"Greg, that place is personal to me, okay? That's the only way I know how to explain it to you. I need it. I will always need it.... It's somewhere I can catch my breath, remember what's important in my life. If you ever try to sell it, I will use you as chum." Her last syllable had been a screech and she'd stood up during her speech.

Greg remained there, sitting peacefully, watching her, which made the scene even more frustrating for Kelly.

"Kelly, is everything all right?" Rafe asked, standing next to her.

"Yes." She turned and gave him a tight smile. "This is my manager, Greg Sanders. Greg, this is my…friend, Rafe. Greg and I were just discussing some business."

Her manager nodded by way of greeting. Greg never liked seeing her with other men, but that was his problem. He called them distractions. Funny, when she was dating him, the surf bunnies he hung out with didn't seem to distract him.

"Do you want to dance?" Rafe's gaze focused in on her, and immediately pulled her from the riptide of fury she was feeling. His grin was heart-stopping. No wonder women swooned around him. That rugged jaw and the intensity in his eyes hinted at danger. Every girl wanted a taste of the dark side.

"I'll talk to you later, Greg," she said by way of a dismissal.

"You have two days to make a decision, then Baywear will move on to their second choice," Greg called out to her. He didn't sound happy. How many times had she brought up Baywear and her desire for that contract? Annoying as he was, he only wanted to help her.

She stopped, deciding she should address him fairly. "I promise. We'll talk tomorrow. And though it doesn't sound like it, I do know how hard you worked for this. But I'm not just going to sign on the dotted line anymore. It's important for you to understand that. I need to think about what it is I want for the future."

Greg frowned.

Kelly took Rafe's hand and told him, "Tonight, we party."

Greg mumbled something, but she couldn't hear him over the growing din of noise.

Last Resort had been turned over to the California Tan team, and they'd decorated it as a colorful, twinkling paradise. There were lights, food and plenty of giveaways. The party planners had even hired bikini-clad girls to dance inside giant plastic balls that rolled around on the surface of the pool. They spun into one another like some kind of bubble derby.

Everything organized about these parties was to entice buyers to pick up loads of product. Many guests at these events were circuit sponsors. If it wasn't for them, Kelly would be counting pennies and still working at her local surf shop. Her parents were well-off, but she and her sister had always been determined to make it on their own.

The Beach Bums band was set up on a makeshift stage. One of their best-known ballads filled the air.

Rafe held her loosely and she slipped her arms around his neck. Emboldened by his voice mail message left for her sister, Kelly felt totally confident. She opened her mouth to tell him the truth, but his gaze scorched her. Pressing herself into him, she laid her cheek on his chest.

"Things seemed heated when I walked up," he said.

She didn't want to talk about Greg. She had a lot to think about and right now all she really wanted to do was lose herself in Rafe. Being here with him, like this, gave her an unexpected sense of calm. It was strange, given they'd just met face-to-face, that he should feel like home to her. She had that same feeling about Last Resort, but it was as if he were the missing piece of the puzzle.

For a few seconds she thought about what it would be like to settle down with someone like Rafe. To give up the travel, the competitions, the adrenaline rush.

Already she was making a home for herself on the island—a home Rafe completed with his mere presence. Of course, she couldn't actually say that to him. The poor guy would freak and run away faster than a cheetah.

"Sorry, didn't mean to interfere with your business," Rafe said apologetically.

"No. That's how Greg and I talk over things these days. He gets on my nerves, and I'm sure I do the same to him."

"From the way he looked at you, the two of you are more than friends." His tone was guarded, cautious.

Lifting her head, she met his gaze. His face was a blank mask.

"We were, a long time ago. But that proverbial boat launched and sank almost simultaneously. We're better business partners. This is nice," she said as she rubbed her cheek against his chest.

"It is." They swayed together perfectly in tune with each other.

She must tell him the truth, Kelly thought. This would be a good time. Maybe in public he wouldn't get upset at her for her deception about Mimi.

"Rafe, there's something I want to talk to you about." She kept her head down, too much of a coward to look him in the eye.

"I have something I need to talk to you about, too," he said, "but let's wait until we're alone. I really just want to enjoy—uh—hanging out with you."

Don't give in to temptation. Be honest with him and rip the bandage off.

But his hands stroked the base of her spine and she gave a happy sigh. One night with Rafe might be the only one she ever had. Realistically, once he did know the truth, he might not forgive her.

It was selfish and stupid, she admitted, but she'd dreamed about him for so long. Never knowing how it felt to—

"Hey, stop hogging the marine." A brunette—one of the California Tan girls—interrupted their dance.

Oh, come on. The image of punching the girl's cute, perky nose filled Kelly with a giddy type of euphoria.

Unfortunately, the consequent lawsuit accompanied by an arrest record and plastic surgery bills would not.

"Marine, am I hogging you?" Kelly leaned back, gazing sweetly at Rafe.

A boyish grin spread across his face. "Oh, no. I'd say it's me who's hogging you." He kissed her softly on the lips.

Hissing in a breath, it took her a moment to register the contact. Then his tongue slid across her teeth and she was lost.

He deepened the kiss, and her body rocked forward. The length of hardness against her belly sent her senses reeling. His hands pressed into her lower back and she had an urge to wrap herself around him.

"Whatever!" The brunette stormed off, her high heels clicking against the wooden dance floor.

"I don't think she's very happy with either of us," Kelly murmured against his lips.

"Don't care. Thanks, by the way, for the save."

Was the kiss a save? Was it simply for show?

"Rafe, I'll always be happy to rescue you from the evil half-naked bikini witches of the world."

The music changed to a faster beat, but they kept moving slowly, their arms around each other.

"That kiss—it…" He paused, as if he had to choose his words carefully.

"Was in the moment and it was nice," she finished for him. And it gave him the out. Though he'd made a good attempt to reach her sister and explain how he now felt, he didn't know that she knew that.

"Very nice," he said. "But I meant for it to be a quick peck. Then our lips met and I lost control. I'm sorry."

He didn't look apologetic; if anything, his blue eyes blazed hotter.

Kelly smiled. "Don't you dare apologize, Rafe. I enjoyed it every bit as much as you did."

"But your sister," he said sadly.

Happily, it was exactly as she thought. "Rafe, there's a connection between us. You know, stuff happens sometimes. We went with it. Don't be upset."

The last thing she wanted was for him to regret their first kiss.

"I'm not upset, that's kind of what I wanted to talk to you about, and I think maybe we shouldn't wait. Do you mind if we take a walk on the beach?"

It felt as if the ground had dropped out from beneath her and she rebounded again.

This is it. Tell him.

Her mouth went dry and her heart skipped a beat. Taking his hand, she led him away from the party. She slipped off her heels and waited while he took off his shoes and rolled up his jeans. Then they walked side by side across the sand.

"I'm trying to get in touch with your sister but she won't return my calls." He exhaled the words on a long breath as they neared the water.

"Oh? I told you, right? That when she gets on a shoot, time flies. She's the worst at returning calls, texts and emails." That was true at least. "Perhaps I can help."

He laughed. "I don't think so. I'm not going to say too much right now. I need to speak to your sister first. It's the right thing to do. But I wanted you to know that kiss was more than a save to me. I'd like to do it again."

Kelly blushed with the news.

"Hmm. Me, too—a lot," she said.

He squeezed her hand. "But that can't happen until I reach your sister and explain."

"Got it," she said, though her mind raced to find a way to solve this situation. If she told him the truth now, he might never want to talk to her again. That would break her heart. If she let him get to know her, the real her, maybe he wouldn't get so mad when the truth came out. "You're an honorable guy. I kind of adore that about you."

At least one of them should be honorable.

"Yeah, I'm not big on games and lies," he said. "The truth is important to me. I have a code I live by."

Kelly couldn't help it. Each word ripped at her heart. "I agree with you to a certain extent, but sometimes white lies can help protect someone from harsh realities. Or they can cushion a terrible blow. I mean, the person needs to have a great reason for lying, but I think sometimes it's necessary."

He shrugged. "I'll take your word on that. Should we go back and join the others?"

The idea of him being mauled by more women was too much for her. "I'm tired of the noise, and I really don't want to deal with Greg anymore," she answered frankly. "How would you feel about watching a movie?"

One golf-cart ride later and they'd arrived at the side entrance to the main building and quickly made it to her suite.

"I'm going to change out of this dress—I'll be back in a minute," she told him.

Tempted to run, she forced herself to walk casually to her bedroom. Once she closed the door, she hurried to her closet.

What am I doing?

Seducing Rafe.

Was she?

Never in her life had she been so unsure of herself. Tackling big waves was a lot easier than relationships. He wanted to wait until he talked to Mimi, but who knew when that would ever happen?

Kelly would have to figure out how to contact her sister and right away. Mimi might not like the subterfuge, but she was also a romantic—one of the reasons she fell in love three or four times a month. Surely, she'd understand Kelly's predicament.

Determined to try again to clear the air with Rafe, Kelly chose her outfit carefully.

She picked the hanger with her favorite white eyelet halter. And digging deep in the bottom shelf of her dresser drawer, she found a white wraparound skirt to match the top.

Five minutes later she pulled her curls into a ponytail, slapped some lip gloss on her lips and decided she was good to go.

Kelly came out of her bedroom to find the television on.

"Supermodel Mimi Callahan was seen frolicking on the shores of a private Malibu beach with her new love, actor Sebastian Lockwood. These two were also seen kissing at the hot new club LaDon last night. Two of the most beautiful people in the world—could this be true love?" The announcer smiled broadly and gave a fake wink as the entertainment show moved on to the next segment.

Rafe shook his head.

"You must be upset. I'm sorry," Kelly said softly. She reached for the remote and turned off the television.

Why did this have to happen tonight?
Tell him the truth.

Rafe faced the expanse of glass that framed the ocean, so she couldn't see his expression. "We can watch a movie tomorrow or the next day," she offered. "You probably don't want anything to do with the Callahan girls. I get it."

"No." The word sounded strangled.

Kelly's heart tightened painfully in her chest. He cared for Mimi, and now he was crushed. As much as Kelly had hoped she might fill in for her sister, she should have known no man got over Mimi that fast. Still, she ached to go to him and take him into her arms and offer comfort.

It was her stupid fault for doing all this in the first place. For making him think that Mimi cared about him when in truth her sister probably didn't even remember who he was. Men were accessories for her. As easily cast aside as a pair of cheap costume earrings. She would fall madly and hopelessly in love with a guy, and then, in a matter of days or weeks, she moved on to the next one.

"I won't make excuses for her, but she's never been one for any type of long-term commitment. I... We should, um—"

Rafe turned around and the big smile on his face shocked her.

"What..." The words wouldn't form in her mouth.

"I'm relieved." He chuckled and walked over to where she was standing. When he looked down at her, she couldn't help noticing that there was something about his eyes, but she couldn't place it. "I've been feeling so guilty, Kelly."

"Why would you feel guilty?" She put her hand on his arm. She needed to touch him. It was as if his body called to her. The more she tried to stay away, the louder the calling.

Rafe gave her a lopsided grin and held her hand.

"Since I've met you, I couldn't even remember what your sister looked like. You're so beautiful and kind. And I wanted you in a way I never have any woman before."

Kelly chewed on the inside of her lip, a nervous habit she'd developed in childhood.

He stepped closer and gently held her face in his hands. He leaned in and placed a light kiss to her lips.

Gasping at how aroused his kiss made her feel, her first instinct was to throw herself at him, instead he must have misread her surprise.

Rafe frowned. "I apologize. I got carried away...."

He wanted her. Now.

Me. Not Mimi.

"Oh, you're not wrong at all. I feel the same way. I've been feeling guilty, too."

For more reasons than he might guess.

Tell him the truth.

Not now. Let him get to know me and then I'll explain. We'll laugh about how silly it all was.

No. She had to tell him the truth before they went any further.

"Rafe—"

But then his lips captured hers in a hungry kiss. And a small sigh escaped from her, allowing him to deepen the kiss as he took her into his arms. Warmth spread through her limbs, making a direct line to her core.

When his fingers stroked her cheek, her jaw and moved lower, she lost all sense of what was around her.

As their tongues danced together, she wasn't sure which one of them moaned first, but as she ran her hands over his taut chest and shoulders, his hard erection tempted her to reach down.

Capturing her hands, he ended the kiss and took a step back. He gave her that boyish grin again. "I think we need to take a breather."

Instantly disappointed, Kelly wondered if maybe he didn't want her as badly as she'd thought. "Sorry, I guess I was the one who got carried away. I, uh…" Humiliated, she found her fingernails the most interesting things in the world.

Reaching out for her, he lifted her chin with his finger. "I do want you," he said, his voice a low growl. Taking a deep, steadying breath, he cleared his throat. "In every way I can have you."

Happiness filled Kelly from the tips of her toes all the way to her blond ponytail. "Then?"

He took her hands in his. "Call me old-fashioned, but I want to take it slow." He stared at her deeply, giving her another devastating smile. "Okay, not exactly slow. But I want you to understand that you aren't my second choice or a rebound. You're it. I was attracted to your sister, but you and I have— I don't even know how to describe it."

"A connection," she suggested.

"Right. And I want to take you out on dates and, um, woo you."

Kelly burst out laughing.

He frowned, clearly unimpressed with her reaction. "Do you have a problem with that?"

"No, sir. I'm all about the wooing. But I was think-ing we've had lunch and dinner together. We went to a party and strolled on the beach. That's like four dates already." She batted her lashes at him.

Rafe nodded. "I like a woman who isn't afraid to go after what she wants."

"That's me," she said. "You don't go after thirty-foot waves if you're a coward."

But you are. You should tell him the truth.

"Hmm. I'm thinking a swim might be good," he said.

"Now?"

"C'mon, it'll be fun." His lazy grin curled her toes. Fine, if he wanted to swim, she'd swim. Maybe he was right about slowing down, but she didn't want to.

"On second thought, that's a great idea, Rafe. I'm in," she told him, and stripped off her top and skirt, prancing right into the water.

6

RAFE'S GAZE WAS glued to Kelly as she dived naked into the sea. Slack-jawed, he couldn't remember a lovelier or more erotic sight. She was exquisite, pure and natural from her shapely legs to her well-toned ass. When she surfaced, she pulled the band from her hair and the mass of heavenly waves fell around her shoulders.

Lifting her arms up toward the moon, she posed waist-deep in the water. He was no exhibitionist, but he wasn't stupid. She'd offered him a gift, and he would not turn it down.

In seconds, he'd stripped and followed her into the sea. The temperature was several degrees cooler than earlier in the day, but heat suffused his body as he neared her.

"This is where I live," she said, looking lovingly at the sky. "The moon gives the gift of waves, and I give her unconditional love." Her tone of voice gave him serenity and a piquant desire. He knew she must be part sea nymph just from the way she rode the waves. His cock twitched as he imagined her riding him wild and free.

He clenched his jaw, desperate to regain control even as the water pushed him toward her. "I didn't think the moon was a woman. I've always heard there was an old man in the moon."

She shook her head, smiling. "No, only a woman could do something this magical."

"You have a point." He believed it because he could hear the unconditional acceptance of it in her voice. Exotic, alluring and yet utterly open and captivating. Just like her. In that instant, he realized he understood her better than he ever would her sister, despite all the wonderful letters. "I get the unconditional part. Probably sounds crazy comparing the military to the ocean and the moon, but I feel the same way about the corps. The corps made me the man I am today. It made me a man, period." Would she really understand his linking her feminine mystery to his devotion to the Marines?

"Right. The Marines is a part of you, like the moon and sea are a part of me." She glanced over her shoulder. The light of the orb's reflection cast an almost supernatural glow along her skin.

He wanted to touch her, but he was almost afraid to spoil the mood. The water eddied between them. Dragging them closer yet edging them apart, like two magnets, attracting and repelling. Her smile invited him to tell her anything.

And damn if he didn't want to. "I was safer in the corps than hanging out at home. Like a lot of my buddies, I was a screwed-up teen with two choices—jail or the military. My dad was pretty set on what choice I should make. He and my mom had done their best, but I was a hardheaded brat. Signing up with the Marines was one of the best decisions I ever made. A year after

I joined, I was going to college online and serving in Afghanistan."

"What did you study in school?" she asked.

He wanted to see her face clearly, but a few wayward strands of her hair blocked his view.

"Business. My former captain and I have a security firm we began last year. I work on the books with another friend of ours, and Will runs the day-to-day operation."

"Wow. I was already impressed by you, but you are one *awesome* dude." Her light tone echoed a far more profound admiration.

He laughed. "You are such a surfer girl."

"Never pretended to be anything different." She lifted her shoulders as an innocent gesture. "I felt brave when I walked out here. Now, I'm nervous."

"Me, too," he said honestly. "This was all so fast. I just want to make sure that you understand that I meant what I said. This has nothing to do with your sister. This is all about you and me."

She reached out to him then. Outlined by the enormous glow of the moon behind her, he could see the need that burned in her eyes. Pert breasts greeted him with tight pink nipples begging for attention.

"Beautiful," he said reverently.

Her eyes traveled from his face on down to his pelvis, his want for her evident.

"Yes, it is."

Sucking in a breath, he touched her.

"Mine," he whispered before his mouth claimed hers in a searing kiss.

He was so engrossed in tasting her that he didn't notice the wave until it crashed down on top of them.

His injured leg gave out and they both slipped beneath the water.

Kelly held on to him and he pushed with all his might. The strain on his leg sent a stab of pain into his hip and back, but he managed to push her above the surface. She helped him in turn, and they both sputtered and coughed.

"That was fun," she said, giggling.

Rafe winced. The pain in his hip and leg released fresh agony with every new wave that slammed into them.

She stopped laughing. "Oh, no, this is too much for your injuries. That's what I get for trying to be romantic and forcing you to make out with me in the ocean."

He wanted to do a lot more than just make out. "The leg is fine," he lied. "And, I'm going to show you romance." Ignoring the pain, he wrapped her in his arms and lost himself as his mouth joined with hers.

Cupping her breast, he thumbed her nipple. She moaned his name in response and though Rafe didn't think it possible, his erection grew harder.

"Kelly!" A voice penetrated from the darkness, abruptly ending the sensual haze she felt she was in.

"Kelly, is that you?" the man persisted in a French accent, calling for her again.

Rafe grabbed her hand, trying to reassure her. Whatever this was, it didn't sound good.

"What's wrong?" Kelly asked dreamily.

"Are you okay?" the man asked.

Rafe didn't know who this guy was, but murder crossed his mind.

"This is so not happening," she said through gritted teeth. "Adrien, I'm fine. This isn't a good time."

"I can see that, but it's an emergency. Some woman is on the phone and she's crying hysterically. Something about your papa. Sounds important, but I do not understand a word she is saying."

Rafe could see the tension in Kelly's face. The humor and desire had gone out of her expression as though she'd been struck by a gale-force wind. To him she said, "I can't believe this. I'm so sorry. I don't know what's going on, but I have to check."

Then to Adrien she yelled, "Tell her I'll be right there."

"Of course, let's go. It's an emergency. Tell me what I can do to help." Rafe forced his leg to cooperate, while trying to shield her nudity from the guy on the beach. Rafe barely relaxed his vigilance until the shadowy figure sprinted off toward the main building.

"This might take a while if it's who I think it is," she said apologetically. She found his shirt, which he'd left just beyond the water's reach, and slipped it on. That was a sight, with her beautiful, tanned legs poking out the bottom of the white cotton.

"No problem. I should head back to my bungalow." Rafe shoved on his jeans, which wasn't easy since his leg was aching. Tiny, hot needles of pain burned deep in the muscles. "I'll see you tomorrow for the—what is that class called?"

"Pilates." She smiled but it didn't quite make it as far as her eyes.

Rafe leaned forward and kissed her forehead. "I'm being serious, let me know if you need help."

"Thanks," she said as she gave him a quick hug and sprinted away.

In contrast, he limped toward his room and grimaced.

At this rate, cold showers might become a part of his regular routine.

"Mom, stop crying. Everything is fine. You know Dad will pop back up at the house tomorrow. He always comes home to you." Of all the nights for her father to take off on one of his little adventures—if he were here, she'd—

"This time is different," her mother insisted. "He didn't even leave a note. And Sissy Carpenter saw him talking to that new tennis coach, Samantha. You know how much your father loves tennis."

Her dad loved anything he could do that would get him out of the house when his wife was in residence. Once a dedicated neurosurgeon and preoccupied for a lot of Kelly's life, he'd since retired a few months ago. He still consulted on special cases from time to time, but he didn't see new patients any longer.

Her mom, a former supermodel, decided she was in no way retiring. She threw herself into the details of her clothing label, perfume and makeup lines and kept herself busy with all kinds of commitments. Her father was done with the limelight. All he wanted to do was play tennis and the occasional game of golf. But her mom nagged him to accompany her to one thing after another.

As if to keep his wife in check, he would take off at a moment's notice. He'd leave on the auspices of an important case, and Kelly and Mimi were stuck picking up the pieces.

Their mother's fits were legendary. Most of the time

she was the life of the party, but it had taken several years for them to discover she suffered from depression. Drugs helped, but not when she added alcohol to the mix. Unfortunately, it sounded as if her mother had found the key to the liquor cabinet again.

Through her floor-to-ceiling window she watched Rafe limp to his room. Stupid wave had done more damage than she'd thought. Kelly had been through enough physical therapy to know how long real healing took.

Her mother droned on about the tennis coach.

Kelly sighed. "Mom, you know he wouldn't cheat on you. You said you did come home three days early to surprise him. He probably figured you wouldn't even know he was gone. He's off playing golf with his buddies. Drinking one too many martinis and passing out at nine, just like he does at home."

This drove her mother nuts since she was a night owl who still liked to go out to clubs and late dinners. Even though she was more than fifty, her mom didn't look a day over thirty.

Kelly reminded herself that her dad might be a jerk sometimes, but he loved his wife. He never failed to tell her how beautiful she was and how important she was to him. And he constantly lavished gifts on her as if she were a harem princess. The two of them existed in a dysfunctional fairy tale, but it worked for them. Most of the time.

"But to not even tell me," her mother wailed again.

This had to stop.

"Mom? I met a guy—a great one."

The phone went silent.

"You never tell us about the men you date. It took us a year and a half to find out about Germaine."

"Greg, mother." That was one of the ways Mom hinted she didn't like someone. She always got the name wrong. Not once had she or Mimi dated a guy that their mother called by the correct name.

"This one is different. He's a marine, and so strong and honest. I didn't think they made men like him anymore."

"Oh, sugar!" The Southern drawl always came out after a few vodka cranberries. "He sounds like heaven. I always did love me a man in uniform. Where did you meet?"

That was a tricky one. "Here. He's a guest staying at the resort."

"Oh, how romantic," she crooned, her overwrought mood completely diverted.

"It was romantic, Mother, until your call interrupted what was turning out to be a really great date," she grumbled.

"Sugar, I'm sorry. You know how it is. Your daddy, I don't think he understands how much his leaving hurts my feelings. I really resent him for that."

So did Kelly, in a way. Though he had a flair for the dramatic when it came to Mom, he'd always been reassuring and kind to his daughters. A calming force. The good cop when it came to sorting things out. But Mom was right. He also had a habit of missing recitals and pageants and always showering them with extravagant gifts to make it up to them.

"Hmm, I think it's time you changed it up," suggested Kelly. "You need to go somewhere with a bunch of your friends. Take a mini vacation and don't tell Dad. When he gets back, he's going to freak when he doesn't find you at home waiting to fawn all over him again.

Sometimes a chick has got to do what she has got to do when it comes to relationships."

There was a long pause. "I always thought Mimi was the game player when it came to men. I never expected to hear something like that from you."

True. Normally, Kelly wasn't the type of woman who went in for games. She preferred to tell it like it was. Her parents' marriage had taught her the importance of communicating and sharing the truth when it came to expectations and desires.

Okay, so she hadn't been exactly honest in the way she invited Rafe to the resort, but she'd been nothing but honest with him since then. Except that part about Rafe's voice mail message for Mimi. She hadn't expected the universe to be so generous with the timing of that entertainment report. But when Rafe kissed her—whatever risks she'd taken, they were worth it.

"But you might be on to something," her mother said. "You get back to your date. I have a vacation to plan," her mother said cheerily. "Love you, honey, sorry about interrupting your fun."

"Love you, too."

She checked the time; the call had lasted only twenty minutes. Rafe was probably in his room.

Kelly changed out of his slightly damp T-shirt and put it in the hamper to be laundered. Poking through her medicine cabinet, she found the special healing balm her physio had given to her when she'd pulled her hamstring.

Rafe's letters hadn't done justice to the extent of his injuries. The scars on his thigh, back and hip signified a grislier time than he'd let on. And even with the initial injuries healed, the scar tissue, possible nerve damage and muscle atrophy could set his full recovery back for years. While she prayed it wasn't true, she acknowledged there was the possibility he might have a slight limp for the rest of his life.

Hips were funny that way. If everything didn't heal exactly as it needed to, it was difficult to repair the damage. Her friend Roni had been one of the best surfers on the pro circuit until her board popped up and came down on her hipbone, smashing it to pieces.

It could have happened to any of the surfers. As it turned out it wasn't Roni's day. Her friend was tough; although her limp was pronounced, she continued to surf. Not competitively, but she had her own surfing school in Newport Beach. Not far from where Kelly's parents lived.

Grabbing a basket from her closet, she collected a sheet and some extra towels. It might not be the romantic end to their date that she'd hoped for, but she could loosen those muscles so he could get at least a decent night's sleep.

7

Rafe fell onto his bed a second time as the pain shot through his hip. Meds. He had to find a way to get to the bathroom for them. He tried to sit up, but a wave of discomfort made his stomach churn.

You're a marine, man. You've hurt far worse after a stupid bar fight.

But that wasn't true. This was different. This hurt came from deep within, and the tension didn't seem to be lessening any.

Sweat beaded on his forehead and he used his arms to push himself up. He rolled over and put all of his weight on his left leg.

"Crap," he bit out as he crashed onto the covers. Forcing himself upright again, he tried to find his balance.

"Hey, what are you doing? Stay where you are," Kelly ordered, entering the bungalow via his open sliding glass doors.

"I'm fine," he grunted. No way in hell did she need to see him flopping around like a rabid dog.

Her eyebrows shot up. "Yes, you're fine, Mr. Macho.

How cool. Now, let me help you get comfortable." She did and soon he was propped up on several fat pillows.

"Men," she said as she fixed the bedding and efficiently positioned his leg on more pillows.

"This isn't necessary," he insisted before sucking in a breath.

"Of course not," she replied as she handed him an empty ice bucket. "That's why your skin is green and your face is sweating—because everything is fine. Where are your painkillers?"

"Don't need them."

"Rafe! You're a big tough marine. You fight in wars the rest of us are barely courageous enough to watch on television. Stop being hardheaded and tell me where your medication is. I know they didn't send you home without any. And why didn't you say your injuries were this bad?"

"Bossy." It was the only word he could get out. Damn the woman. She ran around in her cutoff shorts and sexy top as if she weren't the most beautiful creature on earth. He grabbed a pillow and threw it over his crotch.

"Oh, you've got to be kidding me," she said. She didn't miss a beat. "I can't believe you're thinking about sex when your body is seizing up in pain. I can see the muscles contracting. It's got to be horrendous what you're going through. If I could carry you to the hot tub I would, but we'll make do. Where are your pills?"

He liked her feisty and hot-tempered. She came across as so laid-back about everything else.

"Bathroom. In my shaving—" Before he could say the word *kit* she was back with the drugs and a glass of water. After reading the directions, she handed him two pills, one a muscle relaxer, the other for pain.

"I swallow these and I'm out for the night," he warned. Didn't she see he needed relief of another kind?

She shook her head as if she'd lost all patience with him. "I am not having sex with you tonight, Marine. You're in too much pain. Maybe that's what you're into, but not me." She paused as if she were considering something. "Hmm, fine. Every girl likes a little spanking now and then, and tying someone up can always be fun."

Wicked, desirable…

"You're killing me," he groaned. His erection was as painful as his leg.

She bit back a smile and winked at him.

"If you're a good boy and do what I say, nurse Kelly might see to your other needs. But first, you swallow the pills."

There was hope. So at this point he'd do anything to see her sitting on top of him. To hell with the taking it slow.

"I see that look in your eyes, Marine," she said as he took the pills. "I'm going to leave your pillow in place, so you feel as though your manhood is protected. But I'm rubbing this lotion, really more a liniment, on both legs. It will help those muscles relax faster than you could ever expect."

Rafe almost said something rude about a part of his body she could massage that would bring instant relief but stopped himself. He was a gentleman and she was right. He wouldn't be up to par tonight, no matter how much he might wish it so. And when he did make love to her, he promised himself, it would be something she would never forget.

"I'll start with the front of your legs, but we need to get these boxers off so I can get this salve into your hip."

He'd thrown on the underwear after peeling off his wet jeans.

She reached for the waistband, but he held up a hand.

"I can do it." He waved her away.

The pain was far from gone, but the meds worked quickly enough that he could roll down his boxers and shove them off without assistance. Taking care of him was sweet, but Rafe didn't want a nursemaid.

"Talented. Now turn to the left." She placed a couple of towels on the flat sheet.

He thought she was going to be far more impressed with him undressing himself, particularly given the aroused state of his cock and the amount of total pain he was in. He wanted to impress her. And getting laid up by a teeny-tiny wave definitely wasn't that impressive. A foggy dimness filled his brain.

No. He wanted to—

His eyes drooped and he forced them open. He didn't want to miss a moment of her touching him, as painful as that might be for him. He had learned earlier just how strong her gentle hands could be. "Two massages in one day," he said drowsily. "I'm really starting to like this place. And I really like you and not just because you're so beautiful it makes my heart ache sometimes with wanting to touch you."

She sucked in a breath.

"What's wrong?" he asked.

What did I say?

He couldn't remember. Confusion blurred his mind.

Thankfully, her magic hands kept easing the tension in his leg.

"I like you, too," she said. "That's why I have to be honest about something."

"You can tell me anything, baby." As his eyes drifted closed, he tried to focus on her words.

8

SITTING UP ON her bed in the early morning hours, Kelly listened to the ocean. Yawning, she slipped her bikini and flip-flops on and went to look outside. The sheer white curtains that kept people on the beach from watching her sleep were billowing. She saw the waves were at least five feet high.

A bolt of excitement ran through her like a runaway freight train. It'd been weeks since there'd been some decent waves.

Running upstairs, she knocked on Adrien's door. "Surf's up," she announced.

The chef mumbled something, but by the time she went to grab her board outside, he was right beside her.

"Tempête," he said in French.

She nodded. "Until the storm blows in, let's have some fun."

Concentrating on the waves would keep her from thinking about Rafe, something she'd done for most of the night. In fact, she'd only slept about an hour and a half.

He'd said he liked her.

While this thrilled her, she knew that whatever was between them was temporary. Once she told him the truth he wouldn't be too happy with her. In fact, she had told him the truth, but his light snores indicated he hadn't heard a word of it.

"Damn." As she shifted the wrong way on the board, it flipped. Tumbling through the water, she tried to get her bearings, which was difficult since she couldn't tell up from down. The board hit the side of her head and she screamed in pain, inhaling seawater.

Smart.

When she finally broke through the waves she quickly sucked in some air before another wave could slam into her.

The pain was confusing her, but she pushed herself to swim for shore. A few seconds later, strong hands gripped her upper arms.

"Are you okay?" Rafe's voice penetrated the ache in her head.

"I'm good," she answered, and he guided her up onto dry land. When her feet hit the sand, she sat down and rubbed at her temple.

Rafe knelt in front of her and stared into her eyes.

"Is there a doctor I can call?" he asked as he wrapped a towel around her shoulders.

"I'll be fine. That's the true definition of getting your bell rung," Kelly joked. "Besides, when Adrien comes in he can always take me to the hospital, but I doubt that'll be necessary."

"The cook?" Rafe asked in surprise.

"Chef," she corrected. "He's like my big brother. He quit his old life to surf full-time."

"Huh." Rafe smiled and said, "I guess you really never know about people."

She shrugged. "That's what I love about surfing. People from all walks of life enjoy the sport. Doctors, lawyers, artists and even chefs," she said as Adrien walked up to them.

Her friend held her board and his. After sticking them in the sand, he knelt down.

"Vous avez pris une tête-bêche."

"Not just a tumble, the board wacked the side of her head," Rafe said.

Kelly and Adrien stared at Rafe, surprised that he understood French.

"Elle a la tête dure," Adrien said.

She playfully shoved at her friend. "It's not that hard." They all laughed. "Though Dad did used to say my head was made of granite. A couple of acetaminophen and I'll be good as new."

Rafe helped her to stand up.

She smiled and brushed the sand off her backside. Picking up her board, she began to walk back to the main house.

"Attendre, c'est mauvais." Adrien stopped her and lightly ran his fingertips along her scalp. When he showed his hand to her and Rafe, there was blood.

She sighed. It'd be another day or two before she could surf again. And it meant Adrien would be checking on her every few hours like a cautious mother hen.

His eyebrows rose, and he looked up at Rafe. *"Elle devrait prendre facile."*

"Nous sommes d'accord là-dessus." Rafe agreed with Adrien's diagnosis that she should rest.

She laughed. "Why does it feel like you guys are

ganging up on me?" And she realized it had been a long time since a guy, other than a friend, had genuinely cared about her well-being.

The past few years, most of the men in her life had wanted something from her. Her manager wanted her safe because she made him money. A lot of the men she'd dated had wanted to meet the celebrities she hung out with while surfing. Now she assumed if someone asked her out, it had absolutely nothing to do with her as a person.

Except for Adrien and, now, Rafe. He'd been out of his mind the night before when he'd admitted he liked her. If he'd been the least bit clearheaded she wouldn't have been able to keep her hands off him.

"Why are the waves so big this morning?" Rafe asked as he sat on a stool in the kitchen and watched Adrien clean the small wound on her head.

"There's a tropical storm a few hundred miles away," Kelly answered. "Will probably hit landfall in the next forty-eight hours or so. And Adrien, if you think I'm staying out of the water tomorrow, you're nuts. I don't get to practice that much and I'm not going to miss out on a chance like this."

The chef gave her an evil eye.

"Hey, I forgot to ask. How is your leg doing?"

"About a hundred times better than it was yesterday, thanks to you. Sorry for passing out last night."

"That was all part of my evil plan," she said, "so I say it worked out just fine."

Adrien pronounced her ready to go.

"What classes do you have to teach today?" Rafe asked.

"The guests have left, so we won't have any classes

for a couple of days." She scooted off the bar stool she'd been sitting on. "I let you sleep this morning, but I thought maybe a Pilates workout for you."

She grinned when he flinched. "It's not that bad, although we could do something really fun instead. If your leg is up to it, there's somewhere I'd like to take you. It's a short hike, and a pretty easy one. But if you are in pain at all, we can do it another day."

Rafe pushed a damp curl off her forehead. The intimate gesture sent a frisson of heat through her body. "I'm up for whatever you want to do, Kelly." His voice was soft and seductive.

Excuse me while I melt here.

Kelly cleared her throat.

"You're in Fiji so you have to visit Colo-I-Suva park. It's a rain forest with beautiful pools and waterfalls. The wildlife is pretty spectacular."

"Sounds good. I'll get cleaned up. What time do you want to leave?"

Though the park had been her suggestion, she was a bit disappointed. They could have just hung out on the beach all day, especially if his leg was sore. Still, she reminded herself of the main reason for this expedition. They would be in the middle of the forest when she told him about her deception—they'd at least have to share a ride home while she begged him to forgive her.

Rafe was a sweet guy. He'd understand.

She hoped.

9

"THIS IS PARADISE, Kelly." Rafe tried to take in everything before him. A waterfall with some of the clearest water he'd ever seen poured into the pool next to where they stood. Surrounded by lush vegetation and a spectacular array of colorful birds and other sights and sounds, it was like something straight out of a movie.

She smiled knowingly. "I thought you might like it." Dressed in a powder-blue bikini with her blond curls framing her face, she appeared to be a forest nymph prepared to do magic.

In truth, she had worked magic on Rafe in a mere few days. The muscles in his leg were improved and his depression had eased. He wanted to get out and move, which had been a real problem the past few months. The doctors said he had PTSD, but he hadn't believed them—at first. He did now. While he was in the hospital, his anger had become hard to control at times, and he wasn't himself. The nightmares that continued to plague him were proof that he'd been far from over his ordeal.

Yet, since he'd met Kelly, his nightmares had gone

from causing him to jump up in the middle of the night to seeing the nightmares but only from a safe distance. He wasn't actively involved in them any longer. He bet his shrink at the hospital would have a field day with that one.

But Rafe was here. And he was with the most beautiful woman he'd ever seen, in a place that a postcard couldn't do justice to. The greenery that surrounded the fast-running falls and pool they were now in was breathtaking.

"There are some who believe that this water has healing powers because of the minerals that make up the riverbed," Kelly explained. "That being said, be careful not to swallow the water. I'm sort of paranoid about bacteria after getting really sick off Dungeons in South Africa."

"Yep, in the Marines we talk about that a lot. Always clean your water. I won't lie, I'm surprised by how soft and clear the water is. You'd think with the runoff that the pool would be a little hazy but it isn't."

"One of the many miracles of this place." Her expression changed dramatically. "Oh, um, maybe you should stay very still," she whispered.

Rafe did as she asked, wondering what was behind him. He'd read that there wasn't much in the way of mammals on the island. Fruit bats were about it. Although there were all types of spiders and snakes.

"Boa to your right," she murmured. "They're usually frightened of humans and head the other way. But this one seems to be curious about you. Can't say I blame it—you are kind of delectable."

While Rafe appreciated the compliment, he hated snakes. In fact, he'd rather face enemy fire than any reptile. When he was young, he'd been fascinated by the

Discovery Channel. His mom and dad had worked two jobs each back then to keep food on the table, and Kerr, his brother, had been in charge when they were gone, even though Kerr was only two years older than Rafe.

One day during summer vacation when he and Kerr were home alone, Kerr thought it would be hilarious to tease Rafe unmercifully with a grass snake. Later that night, Kerr found a rattle, which sounded like the tail of a rattlesnake. Rafe ran and locked himself in the bathroom and slept in the tub. He figured he was safe there until he saw a show where snakes came up through the toilet. It was years before he stopped checking to make sure he didn't see any in the bowl.

"Rafe, you're going white. Are you in pain?"

Get it together, man. That thing might go after her.

As a marine it was his job to protect her.

"I'm fine. Not supercrazy about snakes," he admitted. "Where is it now?"

She chewed on her lip. "Really close to your left side," she said quietly.

Rafe kept his body still and craned his head around to see it.

Crap. He wished he hadn't done that. From what he could see, the thing was about ten feet long and huge. He'd seen them squeeze prey so tightly that they cut off their air supply, and then ate them whole.

"I'd rather deal with these guys than sharks," she whispered. "We have a lot of reef sharks who feed around the coral, and they are aggressive beasts."

She made a strange face.

"What is it?" Rafe asked through gritted teeth. Why hadn't he brought his knife? And why was it that beauty always had some kind of catch? He was in a gorgeous place with an amazing woman, and facing down one of the creatures he hated most.

Damn snakes. It took everything he had, every piece of the marine that he was, to keep from screaming like a girl and running from the jungle.

If his buddies could see him now, they'd be laughing their asses off. Except for his friend Will, who was the only man who hated snakes more than Rafe.

"There's another one," she said as she motioned for him to move slowly to his right. "I'm afraid we may be interrupting some kind of mating ritual. As fascinating as that might be to some people, I think it would be a good idea for us to get out of here," she said, increasing her pace a little.

He took her hand and they moved through the water away from the reptiles. But Rafe managed to keep an eye on the snakes, and he wasn't happy when one of them took notice of them. "How close are we to dry land?" he asked.

"About twenty feet," she replied.

"Close enough," he said as he scooped her up and threw her over his shoulder, running like he had enemy fire on his tail. When they reached the sandy bank, he didn't stop. Those snakes were just as fast on land.

"I'll grab our stuff," he said as they made it to the tree line.

"You can put me down, Rafe. You're going to kill your leg again." Before he could do so, she squeaked like a mouse being chased by a cat. "Uh, scratch that. Run as fast as you can. The biggest one is headed our way. Stupid snake, go away." She made shushing noises. "It's probably trying to protect its territory."

Adrenaline coursed through Rafe as he fast-jogged

down the path to the Jeep and tossed her in along with their things. He didn't see the snake when he turned around, but he wasn't about to wait for it to show up.

Tires squealing, they sped down the trail.

They'd gotten more than half a mile away when Rafe let up on the gas.

Kelly's shoulders shook.

He touched her arm and she shifted toward him, laughing so hard that tears came to her eyes.

Rafe couldn't help but chuckle, too.

"Next time," she said as she worked to catch her breath, "you plan the seduction. So far I'm zero for two. Or maybe we should simply stay out of the water. I mean, is it me? Or did the snakes coming after us almost seem biblical in a way?"

Rafe laughed until his stomach hurt.

"I don't know about biblical, but I do know I'll never go back to that place no matter how beautiful it is."

He stopped himself from shuddering. Friggin' snakes. At least he hadn't screamed like a girl. Talk about a mood killer.

"I've been there hundreds of times and I swear I've never even seen a snake," she promised. "An occasional spider or lizard, but never a snake."

"Nice to know they came out just for me," he joked. "So, you were going to seduce me?" Rafe changed the subject from reptiles.

"I keep trying, but I don't think I'm very good at it."

Rafe held her hands and faced her. "Kelly, you seduce me every time I look at you."

Her tanned cheeks burned pink. "Rafe, you can't say stuff like that."

"Why not? It's true."

She shook her head. "Because it makes it hard for me to keep my hands off you."

"Really?" He was intrigued.

"Yes, and wanting your hands all over me. It makes me... I need— Oh, you know." Seemingly embarrassed, she smiled.

"I think I may have a way to satisfy that need." He smiled back.

Yes, he knew exactly how to help her.

10

KELLY WAS HOT for Rafe in the worst kind of way. The island was small, but the drive back to the resort seemed to be taking hours rather than minutes. His promise to satisfy her need had turned her inside out.

Rafe pulled the Jeep into the circular driveway and stopped.

Kelly shivered with anticipation.

And then she nearly tripped over her feet at the sexy smile he gave her as he helped her out of the car.

Pulling her into his arms, Rafe cradled the back of her neck with his hand. She didn't wait for him to take control. Standing on tiptoe, she kissed him.

Using her tongue, she ran it across his lips. His mouth opened with a groan, and power surged through her.

He wanted her every bit as much as she did him.

Tugging his hand, she led him up the front steps. And she kept walking backward until her butt hit the door. Their lips never separated, instead their kiss deepened.

When the door opened suddenly they jumped apart. "Oh, darling, it's you! I thought I heard something," her mother's sweeping voice said from the foyer.

What is she doing in Fiji? In my house!

Kelly stared, stunned. Rafe had to hold on to her shoulders so that she didn't almost fall over.

"She's always been a bit of a klutz away from her surfboard," her mother noted in her most pleasant voice.

"I think she's incredible," Rafe said. His declaration held a soft warning for her mother to back off. Not many men acted that way toward her mother, who had an ethereal beauty and a strange kind of power that drew people, especially men, to her.

Chalk one up for the marine. Kelly loved his protectiveness. It would be nice for once to have someone on her side.

"Mom, what are you doing here?" Kelly asked as she motioned for her mother to back up so they could enter the mansion.

"I took your advice, Kels. I'm on vacation. I didn't even tell the housekeeper where I was headed. And you'll be proud. I packed my own bag, and I only brought one. Though, I'm probably going to have to buy a few things while I'm here."

Her mother followed them into the main living area.

"When I said that about getting away, I meant for you to take your girlfriends and go to a spa in Northern California or something."

Why did her mother have to be here? Now? Talk about a cold shower without the water.

"You're Kelly's mother?" Rafe asked.

"Yes," her mother said, looking skeptically at Rafe. "And I suppose you're the marine she's been telling me about."

"I better be the marine," Rafe teased. "She's so beautiful that I've had to beat the men off with a stick just to get a few minutes alone with her. I apologize for my rudeness earlier. I'm a bit protective of—of my friends."

He cleared his throat.

"Well, isn't Kelly a lucky lady to have such a wonderful—friend." Her mother smiled knowingly.

Kelly grinned.

"It's a pleasure to meet you, ma'am." Rafe held out his hand while keeping Kelly tucked under his other arm.

Her mother shook his hand and then turned her attention back to her daughter. "I've been to every spa in California, darling. I decided that Fiji would be a nice change. And I doubt your father will think to look for me here."

That was a lie. When her dad got home, he'd call Kelly and Mimi to find out if they knew where their mother was. He knew his daughters were terrible liars. Okay, Kelly *usually* was. But lying to Rafe was killing her—every time she tried to tell him, something or someone intervened.

Part of her wondered if these were signs that she was to wait a little longer before admitting the truth.

"How did you two meet?" her mother asked.

Kelly scoffed and tried to wave away the question. The last thing she needed was for Rafe to mention Mimi.

Catching Rafe's attention, she drew him to one of the overstuffed sectionals. "There's a party tonight at the Bay Breeze. Adrien's band is playing, and they're actually pretty good. I promised him I'd be there. Would you like to go?" she asked. "With me?" she quickly added, as if he didn't know.

"I'm always up for a good band." Rafe leaned over

and kissed her forehead. "I'll let you two catch up. I will see you this evening, Kelly."

As much as she hated to see him go, she was almost giddy with relief that her mother hadn't ruined everything. The door closed behind him and she blew out a breath against her teeth.

Focusing her attention back to the matter at hand, she leveled a gaze at the woman across the room. "Mom, we have one rule. You call before you show up. It's the only rule you and I have, unlike the seven thousand, six hundred and seventy that you have with Mimi."

"Darling, I arrived at the airport and walked up to the first counter I saw. They had two flights taking off within the hour. One was coming here and the other to someplace in the Middle East. I thought this might be safer."

Ha! What a tall tale that was. Her mother could survive anywhere. People always went out of their way to help her. In spite of her modeling days being over, her fashion and makeup lines were extremely popular and meant she was still recognized around the world.

As much as she loved her mother and really didn't mind the drama that came with her, Kelly really didn't want her screwing things up with her marine.

"Mom, this thing with Rafe is very new, and if you wreck it for me, I will never forgive you," she told her honestly. "I know you're peeved at Dad, but you have to lay low while you're here. No twenty questions or mind games. Rafe doesn't like that sort of thing." Or in her mother's case, five hundred questions.

"Lovely daughter of mine, you are beginning to make me feel unwanted." Her mother poured herself a fruit-juicy-looking drink, probably a mimosa given the time of day. Her mother always combined her liquor with fruit, believing the antioxidants in the fruit counteracted the potentially disastrous effects of the alcohol. It must work because her mother drank like a fish and yet looked fabulous.

Kelly took a deep breath. "It's not that. He's special. I've never met anyone like him. And I don't want him dragged into our family melodrama. You wouldn't mean to do it, but you always do. I wish you and dad would grow up. It's dumb that you guys don't talk the way normal people do."

Her mother shrugged. "Normal? Kelly, do you know one single family who is normal? There's no such thing. I realize you girls didn't have the traditional childhood. You were obsessed with surfing and your sister with modeling, but your father and I have never done anything but encourage you.

"And as for this situation that's going on with your father, I think he might be in one of those idiotic midlife crises. He lost the twenty pounds he gained after retiring. Bought a new red Viper, and then he took off on one of his trips. We had three different events to attend and—poof—he was just gone."

Her mother sipped her drink.

"Are you on your meds?" Kelly and Mimi didn't beat around the bush when it came to their mother combining pills and alcohol. Most of the time it only made her more mellow, but if she drank too much, then she could go anywhere from suicidal to the happiest woman on earth—and everywhere in between. That's all Kelly needed—to have her mother running around half out of her mind.

"Yes. The doctor just changed them. I'm allowed two cocktails a day. So shush and answer my question."

Kelly had to think about it for a minute.

"Normal to me is where people communicate about their needs and wants. As far as I know, you and Dad have never discussed his little trips. He comes back, you give him one of your eyebrow twitches with the single tear running down your cheek, and then he runs out and buys you a Mercedes or an apartment in Paris. And then you two are blissful peas in a pod until he does it again."

Her mother sat daintily on the nearest sofa and patted the seat beside her. Kelly went along with her mother's request.

"We aren't like most couples, I'll grant you that. But what we have is okay for us. Only this time, I promise, it's different. I'm not so sure he plans on coming home."

The slight catch in her mother's voice bothered Kelly. "What did you do, Mom?"

"Why do you always assume it's me that is at fault?" her mother admonished. She stared down at her glittery pink fingernail polish.

That was her mother's biggest tell. If she was upset or had done something wrong, she couldn't look a person in the eye. Kelly had the same problem, but lately she'd surprised herself. Though she fully intended to tell Rafe the truth, the universe kept conspiring against her.

"Please tell me you didn't use some supermodel dude to try and make Dad jealous. What are you—twelve?"

"Watch your tongue, young lady, I am your mother. And this time I didn't do it on purpose. I haven't done that in years. You know as well as I do that I never did anything with that other man. I only wanted to get your father's attention. And you were seven—how can you even remember that?"

Her dad had been a basket case. That was how she remembered. He'd hired a private detective to follow her mother. Kelly had been privy to more than one conversation between her father and the detective since she'd often gone with her dad to his work. The hospital was close to the ocean, and when he had breaks he took her surfing.

"I was there. It was hard to miss. Call him, Mom. Ask him where he is. You are too *old* to play games."

"I thought we agreed never to use that word, *old,*" her mother complained. "And for the record, it was the tabloids that made something out of nothing. We weren't even on the same coast and it was a picture from ten years ago when we were doing that vodka campaign." Her mother's hand flitted.

"Whatever happened with Dad, fix it. Pick up the phone and…be adult about it." Kelly was tired of being the grown-up in the family. Her sister acted like a teenager half the time, and her parents like spoiled children. They were all good people but had the emotional depth of self-involved tweens at a slumber party. "And stay out of my way with Rafe. I don't want my family to scare him off."

I'll probably do just fine with that all on my own.

"Certainly," her mother said, "Rafe seems like a lovely young man. The way he spoke up for you, well, honey, you deserve a man like him. He is someone who will always have your best interests at heart. And I know that from only meeting him for a few minutes. After all those jerks you dated, who just wanted to take from you, it's about time."

Kelly couldn't believe that her mother remembered the marine's name. Unfortunately, Kelly didn't really deserve Rafe. Though, yes, she had replied to his letters with only the best intentions because Mimi never would. As much as Kelly was supportive in the beginning, the bare truth was that the letters became as important to her as they were to him.

She'd taken an act of altruism and behaved as selfishly as the rest of her family. He was such a good person through and through, and she was nothing more than plain, old deceitful. If she told him what had happened, then she would know one way or the other if he could forgive her.

"Oh, no! There's some odd notion in that brain of yours and it doesn't bode well. Tell me everything."

"You have enough problems, Mom, you don't need mine." There was a part of Kelly that wanted to spill it so that someone besides Adrien knew what was going on with her. The other part was too ashamed.

"Why don't I try your problems on for a change? You're always complaining about my narcissism. It might be nice to put your needs before mine for once." Her mother winked.

Kelly put a hand on her mother's forehead to check for a fever. "Are you sick? Or on drugs other than those you have a prescription for?"

Her mother smirked and swatted at her hand. "Behave yourself, and tell me what's happening."

Kelly grabbed a cushion and squeezed it tight.

And then she told her mother everything.

RAFE COULDN'T BELIEVE he hadn't made the connection that Kelly and Mimi's mom was Raina, one of the most

famous supermodels of all time. Rafe's dad used to say
she was the only woman he'd leave his wife for, and it
had been a running family joke. His mom would say
Raina was more than welcome to pick up the socks he
left all over the house and cook his breakfast at five in
the morning.

Then his dad would take her in his arms and kiss her
so passionately that Rafe and his brother would make
gagging sounds.

Rafe couldn't think about his parents without getting
all choked up. It had been three years since their passing. His mom had had stomach cancer, which took her
quickly. His dad had died a month later due to a heart
attack. The one saving grace was that his parents had
been around to see Rafe straighten himself out. He'd
given them hell as a teen, so rebellious, and for absolutely no reason.

His mother always blamed it on hormones, but there
was no excuse for his behavior back then other than
sheer stupidity. His parents provided him a good life.
They never had a lot of money, but there was a roof over
his head and he always knew he was loved.

He couldn't imagine what Kelly's life had been like
growing up with a supermodel for a mom and another
one for a sister. Of course, neither woman compared to
Kelly's natural beauty.

The woman was a combination of qualities he'd never
seen before. Despite his being scared of the snakes,
she'd stayed calm and never made fun of his phobia.
Her only concern had been for him.

He also couldn't ignore the kissing. Rafe had dated
many women in the past, but none of them had lips

like Kelly's. The type that sent shivers, the good kind, through his entire body.

Then there was the possessiveness he felt. It was so strong that the idea of another man touching Kelly was enough to send his temper into the clouds. She'd called that Adrien a big brother, but Rafe had caught him giving her looks of pure affection. As far as Rafe was concerned, the guy was lucky his head was still attached to his body.

Rafe acknowledged, though, that when she looked at him, there was nothing but desire there. He'd seen it at the waterfall before the snakes arrived. The connection he felt for her scared the hell out of him and at the same time made him truly happy. Never in his life had he been so—he wasn't even sure what the right word was—for a woman.

Rafe's smile beamed back at him in the mirror as he shaved. Since the moment he met Kelly, he hadn't been able to get the image of her out of his head. She was the first woman who'd ever made him think about promises and possibilities.

Way to get ahead of yourself, man. You've known her, what? Maybe forty-eight hours?

She was so easy to talk to and there was an easy grace about her. He'd watched her at the party the night before. People flocked around her. He liked that the only smile that reached her eyes was when she glanced at him, though. If he could bottle that smile, he'd make millions.

"Rafe?"

He patted his face with the towel and peeked around the corner of the bathroom to see Kelly waiting. "Hey, am I running late?"

"No, I'm about ten minutes early. I needed to get away from my mom. She's just full of advice tonight."

Her hair had been pulled up on the sides, and she wore a little more makeup than he'd seen her in. It enhanced the beauty that was there, but it wasn't necessary.

Kelly rolled her eyes. "She did my hair, makeup, nails." She held up her hands and wiggled her fingers. "And even picked out what I was to wear tonight." She did a twirl in her bold red dress and then struck a pose. He liked the way it fit against her curves. She twirled around again to show him the back had been cut away, all the way down to her hip.

His mouth went dry instantly. All the blood in his body rushed to his groin. He wanted her.

Now.

"You don't like it?" The crestfallen note in her voice dragged his gaze back up to hers.

"You're beautiful." He really couldn't give a damn about the dress. It was the woman inside that had him at full attention. Every nerve in his body was tuned in to her. That bow mouth with the full lips. Her fingers stroking the silky dress fabric. Even the way her right foot turned in, as though a thread of uncertainty coiled through her.

He had to stop looking at her or he'd slip that pretty dress off and say to hell with her friends at the bar. Exploring her curves until he memorized every dip and swell would be so much more fun. Clearing his throat, he rubbed the towel against his face.

"Let me finish getting dressed." He pivoted on a heel. Sometime between shaving and her arrival, the twinge in his hip diminished. His body throbbed but with an entirely exquisite kind of pain.

He dropped the towel on the edge of the sink and paused. He was falling for her. He stood right on the edge of a sandbar, and she was the fifteen-to-thirty-foot swells sweeping in to topple him.

His leg ached at the memory, but his spine stiffened. Life kept throwing these top-heavy waves at him, but he hadn't drowned yet.

"Rafe?" Her voice beckoned from the other room.

Snatching his shirt from the hook by the door, he pulled it on and strolled back out. Her grin kindled a new fire in his blood. "I'm ready."

He only hoped that was true.

11

KELLY SURVEYED THE Bay Breeze as she and Rafe walked into the busy nightspot. A few months ago, after a particularly nasty tropical storm, the wildly successful club, which was big with the locals, had been ripped apart. As she scanned the rough-hewn wood tables and the teak bar that had remained standing for more than fifty years, it was hard to remember the decimation.

Everyone in the small community had pitched in to help rebuild their favorite bar. It had taken less than a week.

She loved this little slice of tropical heaven. The food came grilled, the alcohol icy and the music eclectic. Rafe's bemused expression absorbed everything from the band on the makeshift stage to the pair of waiters in khaki shorts and no shirts.

At the crowded tables sat young couples, old couples and a profusion of Kelly's friends, who shouted out greetings as she and Rafe moved through the throng to find a spot at the bar. "Interesting place," he said.

"It's one of the best bars in the world." She ordered a drink and bounced playfully to the rhythm of the drums. It was an obscure song that Adrien's band played, a combination of tribal beat and smoky jazz. "All the locals come here and it's like a big party every night."

Rafe's gaze roamed the room. But each time he caught her studying him, there was no mistaking the heat in his eyes.

Maybe her mom did know what made men drool.

The looks he gave her made her feel powerful and sexy. Despite the cool breeze ruffling the torches on the deck, the air inside the club was stuffy.

"I should apologize for my mother, again. I *wasn't* expecting her." Like anyone really planned for sudden disaster, but Kelly's mob often blew in like a tropical squall, sucking out the sunlight and lashing the beach with furious swells. At least when she had some warning she could surf the waves ahead of time.

"I didn't realize who she was at first, but I guess it makes sense, given Mimi's choice of profession. Did you ever consider modeling?"

He'd gotten a beer and every time his lips touched the top of his bottle she imagined them against her skin. "No." The strangled word barely made it past the lump of emotion in her throat. Swallowing hard, she grabbed her drink just to keep her hands busy and away from him. "I liked surfing and there are some modeling gigs you can get with that. As for hours and hours of walking, posing and worrying about whether I'm tan enough or too tan? Nah. That and I like real food. Given what I do, I get to eat whatever I want."

A mouthful of beer barely quenched the thirst she experienced. Had she ever wanted a man like this? No. The answer came quickly.

"So, why surfing?" That deep voice of his sent a lovely shiver up her spine.

"When I was a kid, Mom traveled a lot and Mimi was already hooked on the life. Me? Not so much. So I hung out with my dad. We lived in Newport Beach and his hospital was right near the ocean and he'd go in for consults on surgeries and then whisk me out to the water." Her expression became wistful. Those were some of her best memories. Just her and Dad on the beach. He'd point out the waves, tell her which ones were great, which ones weren't. They'd paddle out together and catch the ride back in.

"You loved it." Rafe's voice softened, his head tilted as he watched her. "It's written all over your face."

"Yeah, I guess I never really thought about it before, but I was happier on the ocean than I'd ever been on land. I think Dad got that. We went surfing all the time." She'd always thought of her dad as being somewhat absent from her life, but he'd given her the gift of doing what she loved best. At some point, she should probably thank him.

Right after she reamed him out for playing head games with her mother.

"And competing?" Rafe took another sip of beer.

She could stare at his mouth all day, the strength of his jaw and the softness of his lips.

"Complete accident." She turned away from him and leaned into the bar. He twisted to mirror her pose, and closed the distance between them so that their noses nearly brushed. The rest of the bar faded, leaving just the two of them.

"Dad and I were supposed to meet, but he was stuck in surgery. It was hardly the first time, but I was sitting there, watching the waves, and this radio crew started setting up. And then more flags were coming in and surfers flooded the beach. Turns out a local meet was held there every year, but I'd never seen it. A guy came by with a clipboard, handing out numbers and signing people up. I think I was fifteen? I just decided what the hell, I wanted to surf anyway. So I got a number and the rest…well, the rest is history."

Rafe chuckled, the warm puffs of breath tickling her cheek. "What did your dad say?"

"Well, I came in second and he was pretty impressed. But he was livid with the guy who signed me up because I wasn't old enough." Wow, how had she forgotten that? Dad never got angry, not like that. He'd dressed down the coordinator in cool, precise tones and then given her a big hug, a kiss on the cheek, and insisted on buying her a celebration lunch.

"How'd you talk him into letting you compete?" He rested his chin on his fist, his gaze never leaving her.

"Do you really want to talk about this?" She loved competing, riding the wickedest waves. But it couldn't be that interesting to someone who didn't surf.

"I want to know everything about you."

Her stomach did a little flip-flop. "He asked me if I liked it and when I said I did, he hired a coach—a former competitor—and even got me a tutor for school so I could travel. He told me I was old enough to know what I wanted. Until I was eighteen, he or someone in my family always went with me. It's funny, I don't always remember just how supportive he was that first year." He'd gone to every competition he could, making sure to never schedule surgeries when she had a meet. She didn't quite remember when or why that had stopped.

"Sounds like he's a good dad."

"Yeah, he can be. So what about your dad? What did he think of the Marines?"

Rafe smiled and shook his head. "He thought it was a good idea, but it did scare him a little. I told you I wasn't the best kid—truth was, I was a hellion. I got into trouble a lot because I was bored. Bored in school, bored with chores, bored with my friends. Life never seemed to be that exciting."

"Typical teenager. I didn't think anything was exciting until I entered that meet." Which was true. She didn't like all the usual stuff and while her parents were nuts about each other, they were also nuts about appearances. Competing took her away from that world, surrounded her with other athletes who liked to push themselves as hard as she did.

"Yeah, but I don't think you broke curfew, or rebuilt the principal's Mustang in the middle of the gym."

His self-deprecating grin begged laughter and it bubbled up inside of her.

"Seriously?" She stared at him; his sexy expression gave way to one of pure impudence. "You seem so—I don't know, marine-ish. Straight-and-narrow kind of guy."

"Yes, ma'am. The principal busted me for kissing a girl in the hallway one day. Gave us this long, humiliating speech before marching us inside to call our parents. So I got even. He loved that car. And I took it apart, and carried it inside a piece at a time. My parents really didn't know what to do with me. My brother was a star athlete and went to college on scholarship. It was probably just me wanting to rebel against all of those expectations."

His sigh sounded bittersweet. "The last straw came when I got picked up for joyriding, the third time that month. Dad left me in jail for the night and wouldn't let Mom bail me out. I got lucky, though—the cop who arrested me was a retired marine. He told me I could put all my restless energy to good use or begin looking at wasting my life behind bars."

"So you enlisted?" She couldn't picture him as the bad boy, the reckless thief. He was so damn upstanding and honorable.

"Not right away. For the most part, I kept getting off easy. But Dad told me that I had one more chance. If I got caught again, he'd leave me in jail, period. We got into a fight, the kind where you say stupid things you don't mean. I remember being full of self-righteousness up until I saw my mom's face. Her eyes were red-rimmed and full of disappointment. I had made her cry and it killed me. I went from being full of myself to feeling like a jackass. It took me a week, but I called that cop again and asked him about the Marines. He even drove me to the recruiter's office. We had a long talk and they told me if I pulled up my grades, straightened myself up and stopped treading on the law, then they might have a place for me."

"They gave you a purpose. That's what surfing did for me. I wonder sometimes what would have happened if I'd stayed in my mother's superficial world. I'd probably be in rehab or something." Still, no one was perfect, and she did admire all professions.

"My dad was always skeptical and my being in the military terrified Mom. But they watched, helped when I asked, and the day I graduated from Parris Island, they were there in the stands."

"They sound wonderful." She envied that affection, the fierce way he looked when he spoke about them and the devotion mingling with respect in his words.

"They were great. They died a while back, Mom first and then Dad. But they got to see me get it together and they weren't disappointed ever again by me."

She wrapped her arms around him and hugged him. As bothersome as her parents were sometimes, she couldn't fathom burying one, much less both. "You're a good man. I bet you really miss them."

His hands stroked her bare back. "You're kind to say so, and yes, I do." Several minutes passed before his husky voice whispered in her ear, "Want to get out of here now?"

Hell, yes, she wanted to get out of here.

Finally they'd be alone.

Just then a man nearby cleared his throat loudly. As they stepped apart, Adrien thrust a guitar out to Rafe. "Come play." It was a challenge, and it surprised Kelly. What was her old friend up to? If he embarrassed Rafe, she'd never forgive him. Hadn't the guy been through enough?

The crowd thumped their tables and yelled out encouragement. Rafe looked around the room, amusement and exasperation on his face. Giving her a light squeeze, he accepted the guitar. "You stay put."

"You play?" She stared after him and he winked.

"I do a lot of things."

"How did Adrien know?" He had never mentioned music in the letters they'd exchanged; of course, she couldn't tell him that.

Rafe shrugged. "We were in the gym, hitting the weights, and he told me he had a band. I play, too, so we found out we liked a lot of the same music. I'll be back in a few minutes." He gave her a peck on the lips and her mouth craved more when he backed away.

She slid up onto a stool and kept her eyes on him. He put the guitar strap over his shoulder and grabbed a chair on the makeshift stage. When his fingers strummed the first chord, she held her breath.

12

RAFE SPECULATED IF a full-on blitz would be needed to get Kelly alone. Still, he did want to be on good terms with her friends, and, after spending time with Adrien, Rafe acknowledged the dynamic there. Adrien did look after her like a brother would, and the marine in him appreciated that.

"You said you wouldn't have any room for guests tonight," Rafe said as he took a seat near the chef.

Kelly was staring at him from across the room, her lips parted in the sweetest smile.

"But you said that you liked to play, so I thought we'd put you to the test," Adrien explained.

Rafe had skills, but he didn't play in public outside the base. Or, he hadn't until now. "I know some of the songs, but I'm not sure what I want you to do." He glanced at Adrien's bandmates and exchanged easy nods with them.

"Just pick, we'll follow you." Adrien settled back in and Rafe tuned one of the strings on his guitar. He glanced over at Kelly and played the opening notes of a Stevie Ray Vaughan tune. It was the first song that came to mind. The band waited a beat and fell in with him almost perfectly by the fourth cord.

The enthusiastic applause at the end of the song encouraged him, and Adrien insisted he stick around for the rest of the set. Kelly gave him a thumbs-up and crossed one leg over the other.

Her beauty struck him each time he gazed at her. By the end of the set, the only person he played for was her.

IT WAS NEARLY midnight before they left the Bay Breeze. Strolling lazily back to the resort, they followed the moon-drenched beach, carrying their shoes.

"I had no idea you could play that well." Kelly's face shimmered in the ethereal glow. He'd never forget it, no matter what.

"Just something I like to do for fun. No idea why he dragged me up there." The compliment humbled him.

"He likes you, Rafe." Kelly put a hand on his arm, head tilting against his shoulder as she peeked up at the sky. The stars glittered like twinkling lights on a Christmas tree. "And Adrien doesn't like a lot of people."

"He probably wants me to keep my hands off you," he teased, but there was a grain of truth to it. Adrien had kept Rafe onstage all night, barely letting him slip away for a drink.

"Maybe. But it's just his way of looking out for me." She laughed and danced away, only to turn around and walk backward. His heart thudded against his chest. "But Rafe, the question is, do you want to keep your hands off me?"

He came to a slow stop, watching her as she twirled in place. The air seemed lighter when she was around. Fresh, unfiltered purity took over his soul. His dreams had been filled with her. It was as if an invisible line had been drawn to separate his life from the moment he met her. Life before Kelly and life after.

"No. I want to take you back to my room, undress you and touch every inch of you. I want to kiss you—everywhere."

She froze in front of him. Her eyes betrayed her surprise. Was it his blunt honesty? He reached for her.

"And I want you to touch me and stay with me for the rest of the night, just you and me."

He wanted her on top of him, underneath him, in front of him, on the bed, on the beach, in the sun and under the moon.

"No snakes. No parents. No waves. Just you and me," he repeated.

Trailing his fingers down her cheek, he traced the slender column of her neck, then the rapid rise and fall of her breasts, which swelled above the neckline of her dress. Round, soft breasts and perfect, exactly like her.

She took a deep breath. "Rafe…"

"Kelly?" Erotic images of her twined with him, answering the demands of his body, demands that had been made ever since he'd laid eyes on her, were all he could think of.

An emotion flashed across her face like a swift-moving cloud, but he couldn't discern it.

"There's something I need to tell you." She glanced over his shoulder, unable to meet his eyes. Obstacles. She was about to place another one in front of them. They could never move forward if they continued to let the past get in the way.

"Is there someone else?" Maybe she still had feelings for her manager? The idea made Rafe sick, but better to know now.

"No. Not at all." Her eyes finally met his.

"Do you want to be with me?" Rafe had always tried to be direct.

Her eyebrows furrowed. "You can't possibly doubt that. Though I want to clear something—"

"Stop, Kelly. Whatever it is, it doesn't matter." He pulled her against him. Blind desire roared through his body.

"This is important," she told him, but surrender quivered in her voice.

"Is it about your sister?" Had he read her wrong and it was too soon? Rafe could wait until she was more comfortable with the idea.

"Kind of." Kelly put her hands on his chest, but she didn't push away.

"I'm not going to lie," he said. "I do want you. I've never had such an easy connection as I have with you. There's no way I'll ruin that by rushing things. I don't like that this began with your sister. I wish we could put all that behind us, start fresh. Please, let's leave the past where it is. If I've learned anything this year, it's that life is short. And I don't mean that to make you feel sorry for me. That's the last thing I want. Spending time with you, however that happens, is all I want right now."

That pixie smile of hers pulled at the corners of her mouth. "Quite a speech, Marine." She looked up at him through her long lashes.

"Are you saying yes?"

She nodded.

It was time.

Whatever it was she had to say, he didn't need to hear

it. He knew everything about her. She was sexy, sweet, compassionate, giving and so damn hot. He slanted his mouth across hers.

Her tongue stroked his as he teased her with his quick kisses. His shoes fell to the sand and he immediately picked her up. His leg didn't protest or twinge once—it was the rest of his body that wanted his attention. The leg could wait. He barely glanced up from kissing her to make sure they were on course for the resort.

Once inside her suite, Kelly's soft laugh turned into a gasp as he set her down. She rubbed against his body and her hands gripped his hair. She was not a passive kisser, meeting his aggressive need with a need of her own. She danced away from him, a temptress.

Bound by his fierce desire to be next to her always, he followed her into her bedroom. She presented her back to him and pointed to the zipper. Gently lifting her hair, he drew the metal down the curve of her back. Still holding her dress across her breasts, she pivoted to face him and then dropped the silky material.

He sucked in a breath.

She was completely naked. No bra. No nothing.

Every muscle in his body clenched. "You haven't had panties on all evening?"

"I didn't want to waste time if we ever did get to make love tonight."

If he had any doubts about her intentions, or whether she was truly ready, they were washed away by the seduction in her eyes.

She'd just unwrapped a present for him, and he damned well wouldn't wait one minute longer to enjoy his gift.

OFFICIAL OPINION POLL

Dear Reader,

Since you are a book enthusiast, we would like to know what you think.

Inside you will find a short Opinion Poll. Please participate in our Poll by sharing your opinion on 3 subjects that are very important to all of us.

To thank you for your participation, we would like to send you **2 FREE BOOKS** and **2 FREE GIFTS!**

Please enjoy them with our compliments.

Sincerely,

Pam Powers

For Your Reading Pleasure...

Get 2 FREE BOOKS featuring stories that combine a satisfying romantic relationship and plenty of steamy sensuality.

YOUR OPINION POLL
THANK-YOU FREE GIFTS INCLUDE:

▶ **2 HARLEQUIN® BLAZE™ BOOKS**
▶ **2 LOVELY SURPRISE GIFTS**

◀ **DETACH AND MAIL CARD TODAY!** ▶

OFFICIAL OPINION POLL

YOUR OPINION COUNTS!
Please check TRUE or FALSE below to express your opinion about the following statements:

Q1 Do you believe in "true love"?

"TRUE LOVE HAPPENS ONLY ONCE IN A LIFETIME."
○ TRUE
○ FALSE

Q2 Do you think marriage has any value in today's world?

"YOU CAN BE TOTALLY COMMITTED TO SOMEONE WITHOUT BEING MARRIED."
○ TRUE
○ FALSE

Q3 What kind of books do you enjoy?

"A GREAT NOVEL MUST HAVE A HAPPY ENDING."
○ TRUE
○ FALSE

YES! I have placed my sticker in the space provided below. Please send me the **2 FREE books** and **2 FREE gifts** for which I qualify. I understand that I am under no obligation to purchase anything further, as explained on the back of this card.

150/350 HDL F4VZ

FIRST NAME

LAST NAME

ADDRESS

APT.#

CITY

STATE/PROV.

ZIP/POSTAL CODE

Offer limited to one per household and not applicable to series that subscriber is currently receiving.
Your Privacy—The Harlequin® Reader Service is committed to protecting your privacy. Our Privacy Policy is available online at www.ReaderService.com or upon request from the Harlequin Reader Service. We make a portion of our mailing list available to reputable third parties that offer products we believe may interest you. If you prefer that we not exchange your name with third parties, or if you wish to clarify or modify your communication preferences, please visit us at www.ReaderService.com/consumerchoice or write to us at Harlequin Reader Service Preference Service, P.O. Box 9062, Buffalo, NY 14269. Include your complete name and address.

HB-TF-09/13

Printed in the U.S.A. © 2013 HARLEQUIN ENTERPRISES LIMITED.
® and ™ are trademarks owned and used by the trademark owner and/or its licensee.

He groaned, unbuttoning his shirt and stripping off his jeans. His cock sprang free and he noticed Kelly's wide smile. His ego appreciated her look of awe, but now that they were without clothes, they were way too far apart.

She danced farther away and raced over to bounce onto her bed. Artless abandon and reckless wanting collided in Rafe. He stalked after her, pausing only long enough to grab a condom from his jeans. He'd bought a box earlier in the afternoon.

Kelly wasn't the only one who had planned ahead.

As much as his body insisted he move faster, he forced himself to slow down. This was a moment to savor. She rolled up onto her side, a tanned leg stretched out to him. He caught her foot and eased her onto her back. She gazed up at him with unabashed lust.

"What are you doing?" Her white teeth peeked out as they scraped over her lower lip.

He grinned. "I'm enjoying," he said, and tugged her toward him, resting her raised calf against his chest. He massaged a path back and forth from her knee to her ankle. Soon, the smooth skin of her upper thigh beckoned to him. Teasing fingers caressed the softness there and behind her knee, trailing up to her hip.

"And I'm touching." Rosy nipples centered in the middle of white breasts were a sharp contrast to the rest of her honey-brown skin.

Tracing around her belly button, he loved the way her stomach tightened. Her ribs flexed with an indrawn breath. His palm curved over a firm, full breast and grazed her nipple.

It peaked instantly and she squirmed, thrusting her breast into his hand.

"You are so beautiful." His voice was rough with need. As much as he wanted to dive into her like a starving man, he had to take his time. No rushing. Kelly deserved so much more.

One part of his body disagreed, but he ignored it. Kissing her would be a mistake—the minute his lips touched hers, he'd be ready to drown in her.

Whether he bent or she rose up, he wasn't sure, but her arms now embraced him, her leg sliding across his thighs as they finally came together.

His mouth was on hers.

She tasted of cinnamon. Her lips were warm, welcoming. It wasn't in his nature to be gentle, but he held every wild urge at bay as he tightened his hold on her.

At her low moan, he captured her lips, swallowing the sound. Her next gasp ignited his blood and a sweet heat rubbed along his cock. Somewhere in the back of his mind, the need for a condom buzzed, but he wasn't ready yet.

After watching her for the past few days, he craved the taste of her, the feel of her, and his hands roamed her pliant body. Her nails left wild trails of fire along his spine. His cock was hard as steel. She arched into him, pleading for release.

With a grimace, he forced himself to stop. She let out a cry and began to come after him, but he held up the condom as words had failed him. Her lips were swollen from his kisses and a faint redness from his stubble showed on her chin.

"Let me help you with that." She plucked the condom wrapper from his fingers and tore it open. He shuddered as she wrapped her hand around him; he feared it'd be all over right then and there. It didn't help when she rolled the latex down with a gentle caress. He bucked his hips and she answered the beckoning by straddling him.

"Rafe?" The catch in her voice spoke of emotion, desire, everything he definitely shared. "I want you now. No more waiting."

"Always in a rush," he teased, biting back a groan as she squeezed him at the base of his cock and better positioned her knees on either side of him.

Fighting the urge to sink into her, he slipped a hand between Kelly and himself, and tested the ripe, intimate folds of her skin, pleased as her eyes darkened in response.

"We can take it slow next time," she gasped.

Rolling her hard nub between two fingers, he watched her eyes close and her jaw drop open.

Delicious sensations flowed through him as she cried out and he caught her. Pressing his fingers inside her as she met every stroke, a second cry racked her body. Her pure, unbridled passion destroyed the last ounce of his control. Never in his life had he wanted a woman more.

He pushed himself deep inside her. She rose up obediently, her fingers digging into his shoulders.

Her wild hair was completely untamed, flowing as she rode him up and down. Relentless. Eyes filled with lust, panting hard now, she neared another climax. Stroking her hips, her shoulders, he then cupped her breasts, thumbs tweaking her taut nipples.

"Yes," she called out as she clenched his cock.

He thrust, drinking in her primal sounds of pleasure. Again and again he pushed into her softness, the pain in his leg nothing compared to the burning fire racing through him now.

"Open your eyes," he commanded as he increased

the speed of his thrusts. The hazy, erotic gaze she gave him was all it took to lose himself in her. His body rocked back and forth, joined with hers, until they were both spent.

Rafe tucked a couple of curls behind one ear so he could see Kelly's lovely face.

"For a guy with a bum leg, you're not so bad at this sex thing," she said, and smiled up at him as she curled into his chest.

"I'll show you my bum leg," he warned as he reversed their positions so that he was on top. She giggled as her head hit the pillow. "No laughing." He nipped at her chin and then followed that with a tender bite of her lip. Her eyes took on that erotic haze again.

"Yes, sir. Tell me what you want, sir." She held her hand up in a fake salute. "Is it fifty push-ups or something else?"

This woman had him so wound up he didn't know which way was up and which way was down. This connection with her was far beyond anything he'd ever experienced.

Rafe growled and his tongue and teeth found her neck. "Definitely, something else," he whispered.

KELLY ROLLED OVER, hearing the sound of the ocean against the shore. Thoughts of the waves tickled her brain. With the storm on its way, the waves would be amazing. She sat up. The sun was a pale pink promise hanging against the edge of the sky. Her body ached in the best way imaginable.

Rafe was sprawled next to her, his legs tangled with hers. His face was relaxed in slumber. Her heart squeezed as guilt got a hold of her conscience. She should have told him the truth about the letters and Mimi. She had wanted to but had fallen for Rafe's words about starting over.

She wanted to be seduced and so she let him. How could she tell him the story now? Her mother insisted that she keep it to herself. He didn't have to know she was the one who'd written to him. And he had already intended to break it off with Mimi. His voice mail said as much. That Mimi wasn't remotely involved made it even easier.

But it was a *lie* and he deserved so much better.

"Morning." Rafe's sleepy voice washed over her. She'd never tire of hearing it.

"You are one hot marine." The stubble on his cheeks prickled her fingers. Those whiskers had chafed her inner thigh as he'd brought her to climax time and again. Never in her life had she been with such an unselfish lover.

"Hmm, you are as beautiful as ever. That's an interesting hairstyle, but you even make that work." The sweet compliment carried an edge of wicked humor.

Her hair.

She'd forgotten about all the hairspray her mom had used on it the night before.

She quickly went to check her appearance in the mirror over the dresser. Her hair jutted up in three different directions.

"Ack." She tried to flatten it with her hands, but Rafe's arms snaked around her and she found herself back on the bed, staring up at him.

"Look who I found…." He silenced her squeal with a hard, demanding kiss. She groaned and then burst out laughing as his fingers glided down her sides, tickling her.

She squirmed but only ended up farther beneath him, her legs wrapping around his hips. His cock swelled against her stomach, but he continued his slow torture of caresses and kisses.

"Yes, I think it must be a wild woman from the island of Fiji—I hear you have to kiss them into submission." The humor in his voice spiked the need he'd awakened and she pressed into him only to wiggle as he found a particularly sensitive spot.

Wanton, she thrust up against him, the friction both a torment and a release.

A hard knock on the bedroom door left ajar and a throat clearing made Rafe automatically lunge to block their visitor from seeing her naked. She grabbed his shoulders and peeked around him.

Oh, jeez. What was he doing here?

Mortification swooped up and swallowed her whole.

"Hey, Daddy."

"SEEMS LIKE A nice man. How long have you been seeing him, Kelly?" Her father walked beside her. He wore a pale green polo with his requisite khakis, and his feet were bare. He'd always said walking in the sand in bare feet was one of the greatest pleasures in life. Steel-gray hair framed his suntanned face. His dark eyes were hidden behind a pair of sunglasses.

"Daddy, Rafe is a friend of mine. You had no business barging in on us like that. I'm a grown woman."

The embarrassment and shocked look on Rafe's face would be hard to forget. Poor guy. He might never forgive her.

"Nice to meet you, sir," Rafe had mumbled before escaping to the bathroom. Her hurried apology couldn't possibly make up for leaving him with a hard-on and a humiliating introduction.

She'd hustled her father out of there as swiftly as possible.

"Why are you here? And why did you find it necessary to embarrass me?"

"Your chef directed me to you. I won't lie. I thought you were alone. When I heard you scream…" He stopped abruptly and closed his eyes. "There are just some things a father should never see," he grumbled.

Kelly stopped abruptly and whirled to face her father. Finger up, she jabbed him in the chest. "First of all, what I do in the privacy of my own bedroom is none of your business. Secondly, you don't call, you don't text, and you show up like one of the dawn patrol?" She didn't tack on the "in Fiji" part, because that was implied. Her parents lived in California, she lived in Fiji. It wasn't a quick trip.

Another big bonus to living on the island, it put her a good distance away from the family soap opera. Well, until now.

Mom!

He was here to get Mom back. Kelly's irritation evaporated. As unpredictable and self-centered as her parents could be in their dysfunctional relationship, they did care about each other and were heartbreakingly romantic at times.

"I'm sorry, sweetheart, I hate to be the one who has to tell you…but your mother's left me."

Or not. Kelly pinched the bridge of her nose. "Dad—"

"No, it's not altogether unexpected. She and that

Gunther character have been linked for months—years, really. I retired, like she wanted. I bought the house she wanted. I attend all the parties, do all the things she wants. But how could I possibly hope to compete with someone who *understands* her?"

Had her father actually used air quotes? Kelly shook her head. "Daddy…"

He patted her arm in an assuring gesture. "Really, it will be fine. Besides, I wanted to come spend time with my favorite girl. I tried to call Mimi, but she's with some Italian Romeo and can't be bothered with the little people in her life."

Kelly stared agog at her father. He couldn't have surprised her more if he'd sprouted two heads or turned green. Grabbing his arm, she tugged him into resuming their walk. They were almost at the resort.

She would break it to him that Mom was there, encourage a reunion and then watch as he whisked her mother back home. Kelly could exit stage left before the dinner theater got started. Unfortunately, her mother chose that minute to appear at the front door.

"Carter." Her voice cracked like a whip through the predawn hush.

"Raina." The surprise and grief on his face solidified into an emotionless mask. "You brought your lover here?"

"My lover?" Raina marched down the steps, her silken dressing gown flowing around her like some heroine in an old horror movie. Despite the early hour, her hair was perfectly coiffed and her makeup only accented her stunning beauty. "Where is yours? I imagine you've come here to the islands, expecting to sow your oats while our daughter watches? Oh, Carter, what kind of an example is that?"

"The one her mother is already displaying, apparently." He cut a look down at Kelly as though remembering that she was still there. "This isn't an appropriate conversation to have in front of her. If you'll excuse us, Kelly, your mother and I will take this inside."

With that, Carter gripped Raina by the arm and directed her into the mansion, the door slamming shut behind them. Kelly stared at the closed door to *her* house—her *resort* and sighed.

Could this day get any more bizarre?

13

By LATE AFTERNOON, Kelly was about to tear her hair out. A tropical squall was bearing down on the island, which meant the surf was hopping and so was she, not to mention her staff. They'd done a quick stocktaking, reviewed safety measures and boarded up all windows on the inside and closed storm shutters on the outside. Also, she had to crank up the truck and drive into town for fuel. The hollows on the waves were amazing, but she couldn't get anywhere close to them because there was too much work to be done.

Adrien grunted something about the generator before heading out to distribute supplies. She saw Rafe at one point hammering away with the other guys who worked at the resort, but aside from his heart-wrenching smile, she didn't get to talk to him. She mouthed, *Later,* and he gave her a quick nod as she ran off to do her next errand.

She was lucky to get fuel. There had been a lot of tourists and competitors arriving on the island for the weekend's upcoming surf meet. It would be her first competition after several months. It was the one thing

Greg hadn't griped about when he'd cornered her at the party.

At the thought of him, her phone buzzed in her pocket.

Greg's face peered up at her on-screen and she stifled a growl. "Yes, I know, I need to be on the waves and I will be as soon as I get the resort ready for the storm."

"If we hired a manager for you who would run things, you could be out there now." He meant well, he really did. She told herself that over and over. But the fact remained that she didn't want a manager. She loved Last Resort.

"I'll take that under consideration." She so didn't want to fight with Greg. "Look, my parents are here."

"Ah." The sound of understanding, only not. Greg didn't like her parents. Fortunately, the feeling was entirely mutual, so he wouldn't be plaguing her at the resort while they were there. A mixed blessing.

"I've got to go." She shoved the phone in the pocket of her denim shorts and finished adding the fuel and last of the supplies they'd need into the truck.

In all likelihood, the storm would last overnight or maybe a day at most. But she'd been on the island long enough to know they had to be prepared for anything. Better to be safe than stranded and starving.

When she got back to the resort, Adrien took over at the truck and assured her that the generators were good to go, thanks to their handyman, Duke. They might lose phone and satellite, but they would have power. The winds blew in from the east, stronger with each passing hour.

Trees leaned away from the shore and the choppy

waves taunted her. Farther out, the sweeter swells were just getting started.

"I can't believe you're not ready." Raina, elegantly dressed, stood in the main living area and adressed Kelly as she was passing through. "Dinner is in an hour."

"What?" Kelly had barely spoken to her parents. She struggled to rein in her temper, already fried from the day's stressful activities. "I'm sorry, Mother, what are you talking about?"

"Dinner. Your young man is joining us. He will be here at seven and you've not bathed. Have you even run a comb through your hair today?"

She would not kill her mother.

She would *not* kill her mother.

Kelly counted to ten and tried again. "Mom, there's a tropical storm coming and we're getting everything organized…."

Raina waved away the concern. "I know, dear. The place is buttoned down or whatever it is you say. Adrien made sure we had the emergency kits, flashlights and bottled water. They hammered all day getting the windows covered. Now we're going to sit down like civilized people and dine. Go have a bath or shower, and change."

Kelly opened her mouth to argue, but her mother pointed a manicured finger at her. "Your father told me what happened with Rafe. The least we can do is try to show him that we are a normal, happy family. Okay?"

"Mom, *we* are not normal."

"Fine." Her mother's hands went to her hips. "But we are civilized, young woman. You will show that striking and honorable man what a treasure you are. You may have to tell him the truth at some moment, but by then he'll be so enraptured by you, it won't matter. And goodness knows what kind of horrid stories you've been telling him about us. Rafe has been defending our country. I will not have him thinking we are some kind of Hollywood trash."

Usually her mother's diva attitude would put Kelly on edge. However, she did make sense. Sort of. And when Kelly had told her mom everything about the letters and lying to Rafe, she hadn't judged her. Her mother had talked about doing what was right and moving forward.

"Okay, I'll go get ready."

"Wonderful. And put some makeup on—do you want me to help?"

Kelly held up a hand to stop her. "No," she blurted. "I mean, no, thanks, I'm good. Where's Dad?"

Her mother shrugged. "We will see him at dinner. Drinks are in half an hour, you really need to hurry."

Fifteen minutes later, she shut off the blow dryer and slicked her hair back into a ponytail. Her mother would be appalled, but Rafe wouldn't mind. In fact, Rafe might even like it. He enjoyed making her hair fall down over her shoulders.

Her memory ran to their night together, but she shoved the thought away. If she were to survive this dinner, she would need her wits about her.

She chose a blue-and-white halter dress. The skirt had slits that hit midthigh.

It was easier to take off than put on. Pausing at the mirror to give herself the once-over, she added a touch of lip gloss. Outside, the wind continued to batter the property.

When the waves slammed dangerously high onto the beach, the storm would be upon them.

Twenty-nine minutes after reaching her suite, she strolled barefoot back to the living room. Her father rose from his chair to greet Rafe, who had also just arrived.

The marine's amazing smile was like a sip of whiskey warming Kelly's body to the core. No man should ever look that good. The moment his gaze touched hers, tingles raced over her skin.

"Hey." She waved, slightly nervous with two of the men she cared most about in the same room.

"Good evening." Rafe shook her father's hand. "Thank you for inviting me to dinner," he said.

"That would be my wife's idea," her father remarked.

Kelly scrunched her face. "Dad, behave. Rafe is a friend of mine."

Rafe's gaze met hers, and once again, it was as if there was no one else in the room. No, *friend* did not explain what he was to her or her to him. Something that Kelly was a little afraid to explore. How had she fallen for this guy so fast?

Who was she kidding? She'd fallen for him after those first few letters.

Rafe stepped around her dad and gave Kelly a brief kiss on the cheek. Out of her respect for Rafe, and him doing his best to be polite, she didn't pull him in for the kind of kiss she really wanted.

She leaned back slowly and gave him a grin. "I missed you." It was a murmur meant only for him.

"I missed you, too." He brushed another kiss to the tip of her nose. He wrapped one arm around her waist and tucked her against his side.

"Dr. Callahan. We weren't formally introduced earlier. Rafe McCawley."

"I hear you're a marine," her father said by way of a hello.

Kelly stared at her dad, hoping he got her message to be nice.

"Yes, sir. On medical leave."

"Medical?" Her father eyed Rafe.

"Yes, sir."

"In Iraq or Afghanistan?" her father inquired.

"Both, sir. But I was in Somalia when I took some fire meant for civilians."

Kelly knew all of this from his letters, but she acted surprised. "Oh, you never said what happened."

Rafe smiled down at her. "Not something I really like to talk about."

"How many bullets?" Her father continued his inquiry.

"Dad, he just said he doesn't like to talk about it. Give the guy a break."

Rafe squeezed her affectionately. "It's okay." His eyes stayed on hers. "Two in the right shoulder. Two in the right hip, and one in the thigh. Hit the artery. If the ambassador hadn't been a doctor I would have bled out."

"Son, you're lucky to be walking, having survived that kind of damage."

"Yes, sir, I thank God every day that I'm here. No one knows what a blessing life is more than me."

"That's a good attitude for someone who's been through as much as you have." Her father's shoulders had dropped. He might not like Rafe yet, but he respected him. "Going back soon?"

Her father motioned to the bar. Her parents had evi-

dently already served themselves. She glanced around
for her mom, but, despite her admonishment to Kelly
earlier, she was late.

Typical.

"Currently undecided, sir. I've got to finish my medical leave before I can be recertified for active duty."
A note of worry echoed between the words, barely no-
ticeable, except to Kelly. She did hear it. She'd read the
same thing in his letters, too. Recovery was hell and he
had a lot of decisions to make.

The last thing he needed in the mix was a relationship with a woman who lived on the other side of the
world. No one knew that better than she did. Unfortunately, the idea of Rafe going back to serve his country terrified her in ways she didn't like to think about.
What if he wasn't so lucky the next time someone shot
at him? And for how long would he be deployed? It
might be months or longer before she saw him again.

*That's if he's still speaking to you after he finds out
about Mimi.* She cleared her throat.

"He's come to Fiji to relax, Dad. To enjoy the sun,
the sand and the salty air, so maybe we can leave him
alone about his future. His body is healing, and you've
told me often enough that it takes a stress-free environment to recover properly. Can I refill your drink?"
She squeezed Rafe's arm and moved away, claiming
the tumbler from her father's hand.

"Thank you. Anything for you, Rafe?" Her father
wasn't quite done with her date.

"A beer would be good."

"I'll get us both one," she said as she filled her father's glass with another two fingers of Scotch and a
splash of soda. She opened the small refrigerator below

the teak bar and extracted two cold beers, popping the caps with the opener before handing one to Rafe.

He gave her a little wink. Apparently, her father's interrogation wasn't bothering him.

"Where are you stationed, Rafe?"

"Wherever the Marines need me, sir."

"So you travel frequently?" If her father didn't stop soon, she would have to put tranquilizers in his next drink. He'd given her dates the third degree before, but this was just embarrassing. She was a grown woman, for goodness' sake.

"Dad," Kelly said, by way of warning. "How is your golf handicap these days?"

"Unimpressive. I simply want to know how serious the man is. If he travels the world, you're going to spend a lot of your time waiting or, worse, worrying about each other." Her father sipped from his glass, but like a high-powered laser beam, he never took his attention off Rafe. "It would be a shame for her to get sidelined in the prime of her career. She's one of the top athletes in her sport, ranked third worldwide."

"Second," she amended. Or she had been when she'd started her break. The only surfer better than her was Loni Kalakaua. The woman was a dream on a board. As much as Kelly wanted to beat her, she also admired her. "But I haven't decided whether I'll be touring extensively this year." Or ever.

She liked having a home, one place, with friends and coworkers who cared about her.

"She's an incredible surfer, sir," Rafe said proudly. "You are right, even though we don't know each other that well, I would miss her."

Only Rafe could bat away the pointed questions her

father was laying on him and have Kelly sound like an angel.

And he would miss her. She sighed happily.

"You say that now, but celebrity has a way of making people do strange things." Carter's troubled expression intensified as he looked past them.

"And it makes bitter fools of others." Raina strode into the living room in a completely new outfit. The black-and-silver gown more suited for an awards show than a family dinner. Impeccably groomed, she knew exactly how to make an entrance.

"Good evening, Rafe. Please ignore my husband. He's always a bit ridiculous when he's had one too many Scotches." She offered a hand out to Rafe and he had to release Kelly to accept it.

"I'm sure the two of you can email if you're separated. And then there's this newfangled technology called texting, dear," she said to her husband with one eyebrow up, "where people can let each other know what's going on in an instant, without worrying for days or weeks."

The temperature in the room plummeted a good ten degrees. Carter grunted something unintelligible and gulped his drink. Kelly coughed and stared at her mother. *Please don't say anything. Please don't say anything.*

Raina gave her an almost absentminded wave. "Am I wrong?" her mother tried to ask innocently, but Kelly knew it was an act. "With all the advances today, it's not as if you have to be on the same continent to share a romance. Oh, and there's that Skype. One of my friends has, well, she keeps her relationship going by video conferencing with her lover every night they are apart."

Her father's shoulders stiffened.

Rafe nodded slowly and gave her mother an easy smile. "Absolutely, ma'am. Can I get you a drink?"

"Aren't you the charming one? You should hang on to him, Kelly. He's a keeper. They just don't make men like that anymore." She laughed with a light tinkle in her voice. A voice that had charmed princes and male chief executives alike.

Her father's expression became downright menacing, but Rafe managed a polite smile.

"Maybe we should go ahead and sit down to dinner," Kelly suggested, before her mother said something else to aggravate her father.

Yet she was smart enough to know that the Raina and Carter show had only just begun.

Maybe they'd get lucky and the storm would hit a few hours sooner than expected.

How sad was it that she'd rather face a tropical tsunami than her parents over the dinner table.

What happened to wanting to impress the marine? Kelly wondered. Her parents were nothing close to impressive, and her dad was as grumpy as she'd ever seen him.

She rescued Rafe from her mother's clutches and led him to the dining room.

As they went, she prayed to the heavens that no one tried to commit murder before the night was over.

Of course, if her parents didn't straighten up, Kelly would be the one going to jail for that particular crime.

GAMES. HE'D NEVER come across people who were so fond of playing one-upmanship. Problem was, he didn't understand why they'd want to. In his view, well, at least from what Kelly told him, her parents had made mistakes. But if they just stopped and listened to each other, things would be better.

Rafe wasn't sure if there was a planned seating arrangement at the table. There were only four of them for dinner. He claimed the chair to Kelly's left and deliberately shifted it closer to her and away from the sea of icy tension that churned between her parents. The small grateful smile Kelly tossed him was reward enough.

Silver domes kept their food covered and warm. Glasses filled with ice water sat next to empty wine goblets. He nudged one of the goblets aside and set down his beer while he waited. His mother had taught him that men didn't sit down until all the women were seated.

Raina and Carter were in a staring contest as to who would sit first.

He tucked Kelly into place and made the executive decision to pull out a chair for Raina. The older woman rewarded him with the same grateful smile her daughter had bestowed on him, although Raina's didn't quite reach her eyes.

Her daughter's eyes crinkled at the corners whenever she laughed. She smiled with her whole face. Maybe models didn't want to deepen any lines, but wrinkles, as his mother used to say, gave a face character and demonstrated life.

The surfer girl was full to the brim with those traits. She was everything he hadn't known he wanted in a woman. But their meeting came at an awkward time in his life. A time when he had no idea what the future held and he would be a jerk if he tried to make any kind of commitment to a woman. Hell, that he was even thinking about it after knowing Kelly for only a short time showed he was a fool.

He met Carter's cool stare with a bland look and the two men sat.

Kelly reached over and lifted the silver dome top off his plate and hers at the same time. The fresh grilled fish on a bed of zucchini, carrots and mushrooms smelled fantastic. It wasn't a steak, but after hauling sandbags, hammering up window coverings and trekking back and forth to all the bungalows with Adrien, he was starved.

At Kelly's sigh, he leaned closer. "Everything okay?" He made a show of flipping out his napkin.

She shook her head ever so slightly and murmured, "Dad hates fish."

So they'd upset her with their sniping. More than likely her mother had chosen the menu so that it would cause her father to lose his temper. Rafe also wasn't terribly thrilled with their choice of battlegrounds, either. Kelly didn't deserve to be stuck in the middle of a private tug-of-war.

He picked up his fork and knife. "I love fish," he announced with a smile. Personally, he didn't give two figs about fish. He was a beef kind of guy, but Kelly's relieved grin told him he would eat every bite and he would enjoy it, no matter what it tasted like.

"Wonderful." Raina nodded approvingly and sent her husband a definite look of victory as she lifted the silver dome off her own plate. The meal was a silent one and Carter didn't bother to uncover his plate; instead, he sat there nursing his Scotch.

Kelly tried several times to open the conversation,

but she was rebuffed by her parents' single-syllable answers.

Rafe cut into his fish but remained focused on her. Her parents could erect the former Berlin Wall at the dinner table if they wanted; metaphorically, he was moving her to Switzerland.

"So Adrien mentioned the storm could be bad, but probably won't be. Is that right?" He tacked a question onto it to pull Kelly out of the quiet, miserable shell she'd retreated into.

"If the storm hits the island head-on, which it almost always does, it'll be very bad for a few hours and then blow out. However, if it glances by the island and swings around, it won't be as bad, but will last longer."

"Which are we rooting for? Direct hit?" The fish tasted pretty good. Light and flaky, and he detected some kind of citrus and a spicier hint of chili. The vegetables were vegetables, but Rafe pretended it was the best meal he'd ever eaten.

"Direct hits are better even when the ferocity is increased, since they blow past sooner. Most of the structures on the island can take the battering. It's the flooding and rising tides that will be the real issue."

Last Resort was located right on the beach. A fast-rising tide might sweep the place away. Her hand came over to lie across his. "We'll be fine." She grinned. "It's a squall, not a hurricane. Kind of like the terrible twos' version of a storm."

"So, lots of noise, but not a lot of substance."

"Something like that." Her voice gained in strength and she didn't look quite so defeated. He preferred her this way, open and not hiding. He had to wonder if this family tension was another reason she competed so often. She had mentioned traveling a lot on the circuit, farther and farther away from the social circles her sister and mother moved in.

Made sense.

"You want me to stay here with you? I don't mind being in the bungalow, but I'd be worried that something might happen over here." Not to mention he truly didn't want to leave her with her parents. Squall or no squall, the frosty tempest indoors might be worse than the one outside.

The sound of Carter's chair scrapping back ripped through the stony silence.

"We're not done with dinner, Carter." Raina's tone had edged into a higher, more dangerous register.

"As there is very little for me to eat at this table, I'll simply take my drink into the other room." Generals spoke more warmly to misbehaving privates.

Kelly put a hand to her forehead, her gaze focused on her plate.

"In this family, we sit together for a meal and we stay there until our guests have finished. Obviously, you've missed so many family meals that you've forgotten your manners." Her mother's voice wobbled as though threatening hysterics.

Carter made a faintly rude noise, which incensed the woman. Rafe put down his utensils, a prickle of unease creeping up the back of his neck. He got the same sensation just before walking into heavy fire. Situations like this led to a lot of collateral damage.

"You're embarrassing Kelly, Carter. Sit down."

"You know, the only embarrassment in this family is the over-fifty female who refuses to age gracefully, flirting with her daughter's lover right in front of her.

And for the record, you, too, have missed your fair share of family meals."

"Me! How dare you? Running off with the tennis floozy! A woman from the club, Carter? One that every man there has slept with multiple times? Surely, you could do better."

And there it was.

Kelly's fist slammed into the table, making plates and glasses clatter and even Rafe drop his fork. She shoved her own chair back and stood up. "Shut up, Mother."

"Kelly! Do not speak to your mother that way." Carter stared at his daughter.

"Can it, Dad. I've never known two more ridiculous people. I'm embarrassed to call you my parents." She threw her napkin down and Rafe rose, more in support and to protect her in case dishes or crystal started flying. Who needed a storm with these people in a house together?

"Kelly, watch your tone of voice." Raina sounded impressively shocked, while her hand flattened against her chest like some Southern belle in the midst of having the vapors.

"You know what—Raina—I wouldn't talk to you like a child if you didn't behave as if he'd pulled your pigtail and you want to make him pay. You're my parents. You're supposed to be supportive. I haven't seen you guys in forever. And yes, I'm happy to say it's on purpose. There's an exceptionally good reason why I stopped coming home, even for the holidays. If you aren't fighting, you're acting so gooey-eyed you exclude anyone else who's around. You make Mimi and me feel like third and fourth wheels. You always have.

"And you talk about manners!" She angrily pointed a finger at her mother. "You served a meal you knew Dad would hate. You wanted to get back at him because he runs off without you.

"And you—" She swung her attention to her father. "You could have at least eaten the vegetables and potatoes that we all know you love. No, you have to make a scene."

Rafe's head bobbed back and forth as if he were watching a tennis match. His girl was mad, and he kind of liked that she was standing up to these irresponsible people. It made him miss his mom and dad.

Her shoulders straightened, and he could have sworn he heard her growl. "Dad, you get pissed off because Mom does something you don't like and you disappear. Mom, you get pissed off because Dad disappears when you won't leave him alone. But instead of talking about it, you bring it *here* to my island. To *my* home where I am trying to get to know the best guy I've ever met and I wouldn't be surprised if he dumped me after meeting the pair of you. Who would want to be involved in this?" She threw up her hands, wildly gesticulating at her parents.

Tears shimmered across Kelly's eyes and his heart twisted. He put a hand on her arm, but she shook him off, trembling.

"I'm sorry, Rafe. I'm sorry my father is a selfish jerk who can't tell Mom what he wants, and I'm sorry my mother is a diva who uses fake affairs to get even with her husband when he doesn't do what she wants. I'm done with you two. I want you out of my resort and off my island. I don't care if you have to swim to do it. Get out! And don't bother coming back until you've grown up.

"Rafe, you are a lovely man. Once again, please accept my apologies." The last thing she needed to do was apologize to him, but she ran out of the room before he could say anything. He glanced at her shell-shocked parents and grabbed his beer and Kelly's.

"It's not my place, but I care about your daughter. You hurt her tonight, and I'm not okay with that. You stay away from her, parents or not. She doesn't deserve to be treated this way. She loves you both so much, and the two of you just throw it away. I lost my parents a few years ago, and I would do anything to have them back. But I wouldn't blame Kelly if she never wanted to see either of you again."

The front door slammed and he raced to follow her outside. The tang of rain was in the air, but unlike his first three nights on the island, no moon shone over the sand.

He stood still, letting his eyes adjust to the dimness, and tracked her to where she stood by the water's edge. Quietly, with the steady wind ruffling his hair and clothes, he walked up behind her and wrapped his arms around her waist.

She stiffened at first, but then leaned into him.

"You must think I'm a terrible person."

"Nah. I'm just glad you didn't start throwing food— or china. That would have made a really big mess to clean up."

Her watery laugh went straight to his soul. He squeezed her tighter to his chest and kissed the top of her head.

"I hate that they do this to me."

"Me, too. My parents didn't hide anything, which I used to hate. Everything was shouted out right then and there. But now I see the beauty in it. They never built up resentments. They didn't always agree, but they did find common ground."

"You're lucky to have had such a great example of a loving relationship," she said sadly. "My parents do love each other in their own way, but I'm tired of being stuck in the middle. So is my sister. I meant it when I said I don't think either of us has been home for Christmas in years."

She cleared her throat. "But it's lonely. I miss them, even though I can't stand to be around them sometimes."

In a show of solidarity, of respect and of heart, he turned her around.

"You aren't alone anymore," he said, putting everything he felt for her in those words.

And he meant them.

Hell, I'm in trouble.

14

KELLY LET RAFE hold her to his chest, absorbing the inner strength he gave her. He didn't even sway with the breeze that tugged at her hair and whipped her skirt around her legs. "The shrinks always say it's better to talk about it," Rafe said as he caressed her cheek. "I'm not sure I always agree with that, but, in this instance, it may be the right idea."

Kelly still couldn't believe he wanted to be with her after what he'd just witnessed. Her parents were difficult to accept.

"I don't want to burden you with their theatrics," she explained. "You've heard enough."

Rafe kissed her forehead. "You need to vent, though you were doing a pretty decent job of it in there." He frowned when she started to speak, so she stopped. "They got exactly what they deserved, Kelly, after the way they treated you in your own home. You had every right to say what you did."

Kelly tightened her arms around his waist. He'd become her anchor in a rather choppy sea. "You really are the best," she said. "If I were you, I'd be running for the airport."

"I'm a marine. We face the enemy head-on. Now, tell me what set them off."

"There was a story in the tabloids about Mom and this male model. They'd been photographed while they were on a shoot. But the pictures were all grainy and low-grade quality. The speculation ran for weeks that the two were having an affair. My dad was livid. He hired a private investigator. He did everything to find out what was going on, and the P.I. always reported to him when we were at the beach. The guy could never find anything on her. She was flirty, but there were no sordid meetings in hotels or anywhere else for that matter. Dad spent a fortune trying to find something that wasn't there. In a weird way, Dr. Ego didn't think he was enough for her."

"Maybe you should be a therapist." Rafe pushed a stray hair out of her eyes. The wind whipped around them, but it was welcome after the stuffy atmosphere at the house.

"The waves are my therapy," she said, and laughed. "I don't think I've ever told anyone that."

"Hey, I'm the last one to knock therapy. As I said before, I've got my own issues. But tell me more about the beginning of all this. You said your dad couldn't find anything. Why didn't it end back then?"

That had happened the first year after Kelly started competing. It all tumbled into place. Why she stopped caring if her dad was there. Tears clogged her voice. "Mom wasn't having an affair, but she wouldn't tell Dad that. She liked that he was jealous. She thought it was good for him because he did have a surgeon's ego, but never when it came to her. She didn't figure it out that it was because he thought he couldn't cut it when it came to her glamour and expectations and—"

"They obviously made it through that rough patch." The simple words were an affirmation of the fact that her parents were still together.

"Yeah. Until Mom pushed for another party or another event or something more. When Mimi's star rose, Mom's was in decline. But she didn't let it go. Mom never met a charity function, a political fund-raiser, a movie premier she wouldn't attend. I'm sure it has something to do with the adulation she receives when she's in the public eye. Even today—when her modeling career has been over for decades—it's true."

"I gather your dad isn't crazy about the publicity."

She shrugged. "He used to be. He traveled as much as Mom did. He's a specialist and a rare one, so he gets flown all around the world to consult on patients. That's how he and Mom met. The jet-setters. He's retired now. In fact, she was the one who insisted they both slow down." She smiled a little then.

"But Mom refuses to settle down. When she pushes too hard, he'll take off for a few days. Sometimes he hangs out with friends. Most of the time he goes to this little apartment down near the Santa Monica pier and drinks beer on his balcony, plays music. I saw him there once. Lots of peace and quiet."

But wasn't that what Last Resort was for her? A sanctuary away from the hectic pace of the pro surfing circuit, no Greg and no drama from her parents? Only she didn't have to worry about a wife to go home to or daughters that needed her.

She didn't have to go back ever.

"It sounds to me like your parents have to work this out on their own," he said as he hugged her gently. "I'd kick them out for you, but there's a storm coming."

She laughed at the rueful note in his voice. "I shouldn't have blown up like that."

"Families need to fight sometimes. It's better to get it out in the open, and then you can start on healing. You've been running away from your family for a long time. They deserve to know why, and you deserve some peace and quiet. You'll have that now—no more resentment because they know exactly how you feel."

His simple words melted her heart. She barely understood it, but he summed it up so perfectly.

"It's so much easier to love them from a distance."

"Than it is to be disappointed up close. I get that." He kissed her hair again. "I thought the same thing about my parents when I was younger. And in her own way, that's probably what happened with Mimi."

She went still at the mention of her sister.

"Shh." He gave her a squeeze. "I don't have feelings for your sister. I was surprised when she finally answered my letters, especially when I learned who she was. When we met, to me, she was just another model who had helped out with my friend's fashion show.

"I realize now that she never actually told me anything about herself, or her family. After what I saw today it makes sense. But she invited me here, and for that I will be forever grateful."

Kelly kept her face tight against his chest. She wasn't sure she had the strength to tell him the truth tonight, but he was her lifeline and she had to do it.

"Rafe, there's something you should know."

He chuckled. "I wanted to say it first."

"What?"

She lifted her head and stared at him, confused.

Lightning flashed in the distance. She began counting. At the fifteenth one-thousand the thunder cracked. The storm was still miles offshore.

"Without Mimi's support—even at a distance—I wouldn't have met you," he said.

"I don't know what I would have done tonight if you weren't here." Absolute truth. Rafe was her safe harbor.

"You don't have to find out, because I'm right here."

His mouth closed over hers. Tears salted the kiss, but his mouth moved gently, stealing her breath, her sadness and her loneliness.

She clung to him, the wind pushing them together. Another roll of thunder echoed across the sky and his hands glided down her hips. He lifted her and the wind pushed her skirt wide until his hands skimmed over bare skin and cupped her bottom.

His fingers caressed the softness and the lightning illuminated his positively wicked grin.

Her body was on fire, throbbing from his kiss and his hands. He listened to her, he comforted her, and now he pleasured her.

She would tell him the truth, but she needed this. One more time with him. Moments she would treasure for the rest of her life.

"Make love to me," she whispered. "Right here. Right now."

"There's a storm, honey." He glanced into the distance, frowning, but she caught his face in her hands. Everything had spiraled out of control. Little lies piled on top of big ones.

She didn't want that for them. She wanted to be as

close to him as two people could be. "I need you, Rafe. I need to feel you filling me, touching me...."

A low groan vibrated in his throat and he caught her mouth in another slow, sweet, torturous kiss.

"Not here," he growled. "I don't want someone interrupting us."

Kelly knew exactly where to go. She ran back up the beach for the sliding glass doors to her bedroom. Just as they reached the doors, a torrential rain began soaking them. Somewhere between one stroke of his mouth and the next, her dress slid down and his shirt was open. Her naked back was against the glass.

Smoothing her hand across the hard muscle of his chest, she found all of his scars and traced them. He buried his face against her throat and used his fingers between her legs to tease her unmercifully. She gasped at the feel of him pushing inside, but he retreated too quickly.

"You're the most extraordinary woman I've ever met," he murmured against her ear as he drew her arms above her head. The rain pelted down and Rafe's demanding mouth claimed hers. Consuming and filling her at the same time. No one had ever kissed her like this, wanting her to feel his passion for her.

She did.

When he pulled back, she mewed with disappointment.

"Don't we need to do something about this?" He knocked lightly on the glass doors behind her.

"Hurricane proof," she explained. "Wait here. Give me thirty seconds." Then she slipped into her bedroom and dashed over to lock the suite's door that led to the main part of the house. She was determined no one would interrupt them tonight. On her way back she grabbed a condom from the table beside her bed. But when she returned to Rafe outside, he wasn't there. "Rafe?"

Picking up her dress, she slipped it on. Where had he gone?

Stepping farther out onto the adjoining deck, she scanned the beach. She spotted him thirty yards away trying to shield something from the rain. She ran to him.

"Who is that?" she gasped.

"Your father."

"He's passed out?"

The wind and rain whipped around them.

Rafe nodded and made for the closest door to the main house. She followed.

In mere seconds, they were safely inside the resort's large kitchen.

"What happened?" she asked.

Rafe had set her father in a chair and was rousing him out of his stupor. "I heard him calling for you, saw him weaving, heading out to the ocean." Rafe's voice was gruff from the effort. "I wanted to get to him before you saw, before you were hurt even more, but you were too quick." He wiped away the droplets in his hair and eyes and stared at her. "You need to know...I wanted you so bad it hurts."

She stood there, stunned by the emotions overwhelming her.

The silence was only broken by her father coughing and muttering something. They transferred him carefully to a couch in the living room.

Rafe grimaced as he sat down on the edge of the sofa.

"What could he have been doing out there?"

Rafe shrugged, closing his eyes momentarily, his face taut with pain.

She'd noticed all this when he had hurt himself before. "Your leg," she whispered. "What did you do?"

"I ran after him, since he was right at the water, think he was crazily searching for you. Then a giant wave came up and pulled him under. I got there just in time to grab him, but the force and momentum were so strong."

The undertow could have killed them.

What had her father been thinking?

"I had to get us out of there before we both drowned. My leg wasn't going to hold up much longer. I hauled him over my shoulder, but when I got him back on the sand he wasn't exactly steady." He looked apologetic. "He slipped and I—couldn't lift him, so I had to drag him a short distance to make sure we were safe. Sorry."

She threw her arms around his neck and kissed him. "I'm so grateful to you, and I'm the one who's sorry that you're in pain now. This isn't like my dad. He's usually so levelheaded, except when it comes to my mother."

"I heard that," her mother chimed in.

She strode into the living room and picked up a throw blanket from the back of an overstuffed chair. She carefully wrapped the blanket around her husband and sat down next to him.

"You should have let him drown." Her mother smiled and shook her head as she wiped the sand from her husband's face. "He deserved it, but thank you, Rafe, for saving him. He might be an idiot, but he's my idiot." She leaned down and affectionately put her head on her husband's chest. "Stupid man."

Kelly's eyes watered.

Rafe stood and hugged her. He could be so tender. She smiled at the thought of him helping her dad, all boozy and absurd, out in this weather.

Then she started to giggle and she couldn't stop.

It must have been infectious, since her mother laughed as well.

Rafe watched them as if they were all certifiable. Weren't they?

"What's sooo funny?" Her dad's question sent them into hysterics.

Rafe let go of her, but she caught the smile he tried to hide as he ducked his head.

"Can't breeeve," her father complained.

The two women laughed harder.

It was several minutes before Kelly felt as though she could catch her breath.

When she glanced over at Rafe, he gave her a tight smile, then winced.

His leg. What if he'd damaged it more? She'd never forgive herself. She remembered what he said about the doctors telling him he had to take it easy or he could cause permanent damage.

Her smile instantly disappeared, as did the hilarity that went with it.

"Dad, how sober are you?"

At the serious change in her tone, her parents stared up at her.

Her mother zeroed in on Rafe's tight shoulders.

Kelly nodded.

"Carter, Rafe saved your life, now it's time for you to help him," her mother said. "He's in a lot of pain."

Rafe remained still where he was. "I'll head back to

my bungalow. Don't worry about me," Rafe said, but his low voice indicated he was anything but fine.

Her father sat up and blinked several times to focus on his wife, then Kelly and Rafe.

Her mother raised an eyebrow.

"Raina, run upstairs and get my bag, please. It's in the closet." Her father took the bag everywhere he went just in case of emergencies. "Kelly, what's the storm doing?" her father asked.

"More a thunderstorm than anything. It stalled out about a hundred miles in. The winds are wicked, though."

"Good, we don't have to move him to the second floor, at least not yet. You go run a hot bath in that hot tub of yours. Do you have Epsom salts?"

"Yes." The salts and a hot bath were the best thing for tired muscles, which she always had when she was training.

"Put a lot in." He turned to Rafe. "Son, I owe you an apology." Kelly stifled a laugh, because it sounded like "apwowgie." But Rafe's color, which was now paler than she'd ever seen him, was enough to squash any humor.

"It's fine, sir."

"No, it isn't, but I'm sober enough now to see that you do need my help. Do yourself a favor and lie down on the couch so I can examine your leg."

Rafe shook his head.

Kelly was worried. Her dad had on his somber doctor's face, which meant he knew something merely from the way Rafe was standing.

Her hands went to his. "Rafe McCawley, you do what my dad says, or I will give you a taste of what I gave them earlier. Now," she demanded and she pointed her finger at the couch.

Rafe watched her warily as he complied.

"Dad, I'll prepare the bath and help you get him in there when it's time. You two behave."

She took a few steps and stopped.

"Dad, I swear, I'll never speak to you again if you've caused him permanent harm. I care about him more than I've ever cared about any man." It didn't matter what Rafe might think of her for making such a declaration. She wanted him to know how important he was to her. "Keep that in mind while you're taking care of him."

Turning the corner, she paused to listen.

"Is she always like this?" Rafe asked.

"Marine, if she's anything like her mother, you're in for one of hell of a ride."

Rafe chuckled, and she let go of the breath she'd been holding.

"I can take it, sir. I've been through worse."

"That you have, my boy. That you have."

Kelly chewed on her lip as she found the salts and poured them into the bath. While the water ran, she found him some fluffy towels.

She knew the answer to her own question before she asked it. But that was all about to change.

Rafe was her priority, plain and simple. In her heart, he even came before the resort.

Oh, hell. She'd fallen even harder than she'd thought.

Her mind drifted to the secret she kept from him. Once he healed she would tell him the truth. But until then, she would look after him. He had a brother, but for the most part, like he said, he was alone in the world. *Not any longer.* She recalled his words to her.

They both had an anchor to get them through the storm.

She only hoped it would be enough once he knew the truth.

15

KELLY CARED ABOUT him. As Rafe soaked in the warm water of the hot tub, his hip and leg positioned in front of the pounding jets, a grin spread across his face. She'd said that her feelings for him were stronger than she'd ever had for any other man.

Relief flooded his chest. While he'd known they desired each other, this was entirely different. She was as invested in their budding relationship as he was. It was frightening and crazy good—as she liked to say—at the same time. Rafe's main goal the past few months had been to recover, physically and mentally. Though the shrinks thought otherwise, he knew his mind was on the mend now, since he had met Kelly.

And he had hope for the first time in a long time. Many in the military suffered depression after they'd gone through the kind of trauma he had. When he came to the realization that his leg might never be 100 percent, it hit him hard. Though he had many options beyond the Marines, the corps was his life. But if he couldn't go back to active duty…

That led to thoughts about Kelly and what if their relationship progressed. But how would it? With her traveling so frequently and him, if he stayed in the corps, never knowing where he might end up. It wouldn't be fair to either of them to make promises or some kind of commitment, although the idea of never seeing her after this trip was one he couldn't accept.

Rafe had watched his friend Will leave the corps to be with the woman he loved. When it happened, Rafe believed he was a fool. Yet after meeting Kelly, he understood. There wasn't a person in the world he wanted to be with more than her. And he'd do anything for her.

Man, you got it bad.

"Hey, Marine, no sleeping in the tub…." Her sweet voice interrupted his thoughts.

He opened his eyes to find her kneeling beside the tub with a pile of towels.

"You almost drowned once tonight, I'd rather not have a repeat." She dipped a finger in the water. "It's cooling down—do you want me to add more hot water?" She reached for the tap, but he gently pulled her hand away.

"I'm fine, Kelly. I mean it. Your dad gave me that steroid shot and I'm not in much pain."

"Okay, but you still have to take it easy," she said anxiously. "Dad said you were lucky tonight. You could have ripped those tendons that had only just healed. And I agree with him about getting new scans to make sure there aren't any tears."

Rafe kissed her hand. "I'm lucky, that's for sure."

"That's what—"

"No. I mean, I'm lucky the most beautiful girl I've ever met cares about me enough to boss me around and threaten her father."

She smiled as she let go of his hand and then brushed his cheek.

"I keep telling you guys not to mess with surfer chicks. We're all hang-ten and livin' life, dude. That is, until someone we care about gets hurt." She leaned over and kissed him lightly on the lips.

"You know, there's room in here for two. Hell, we could probably fit three or four in here."

Her eyebrows shot up. "First of all, it will only be you and me, buddy. You need to know that straight up. Second, my mom and dad are outside my bedroom door. So I'm not exactly feeling it right now."

He couldn't help but chuckle as he noticed her breasts. Her nipples were tight against her white cotton T-shirt.

She rolled her eyes. "It's cold." Then she grinned. "Yes, all you have to do is look at me, and I, well, it doesn't matter. You're going to take it easy. Now let me help you out of there. Do you want me to get Dad?"

Rafe shook his head. He hadn't lied, he definitely felt better. But he was smart enough to know the steroids were only a temporary fix. At least the pain would back off for a few days, and maybe by then his body would have repaired any of the damage he'd done to it.

Rafe pushed himself up to the ledge of the tub with his forearms. In the hospital, he'd learned how to put most of his weight on his arms to take the pressure off his hip and leg.

He sat there while she dried him off. It was sweet and sexy as hell the care she took with his body. And he couldn't hide the evidence of just how much he liked her touch.

"Give it up, Marine." She kissed his cheek. "We are so not going there tonight."

"We marines never give up," he whispered as he pulled her onto his lap.

Swatting him with the towel, she tried to stand up, but he held her tight.

"I need you," he told her as he nipped at her ear and then trailed kisses down her neck. The pulse there increased.

"But you need to—"

His lips silenced her, and his hands palmed her breasts.

She moaned and pressed herself into his caress.

"Tell your parents to go to bed," he ordered as he thumbed her taut nipple through the T-shirt.

She shook her head.

"I've taken orders from you tonight, now it's time for you to do the same."

She sized him up for a second and then smiled. "On one condition."

"And that is?"

"You know that thing you do with your tongue…"

"Consider it done."

He wasn't sure that he'd ever seen her move so fast.

THE STORM CONTINUED to lash the shore when she woke in the morning. She had no idea when they'd finally made it to the bed and she didn't care. Curled next to Rafe, there was no better place to be.

He slept on his stomach, one arm thrown possessively over her. His hand held her waist and his face was burrowed against her shoulder. Leaning close, she kissed one eyelid and then the other until he gazed up at her sleepily.

"Still dark. Go back to sleep." The command was gruff and sweet.

"That's the storm. It's morning, I need to check on my parents."

He groaned, his mouth barely moving as he said, "Give me a minute and I'll go with you."

"Ha." She slowly, lovingly, feathered his hair though her fingers. "No, I'd rather you stayed in bed so when I return, I can crawl right back in here with you."

His arm tightened. "Stay. Go see them later."

"I would, but there is a storm." After everything that had happened last night, she had to make sure they hadn't killed each other after she'd sent them to bed. That would be really bad for business, not to mention any future family holidays.

Rafe lifted his head and glanced at the windows. Like the rest of the property, they were shuttered. Meanwhile, the rain pounded the roof with heavy drops and the wind constantly howled.

"They're fine, and you know it," he said.

"Rafe…" He wasn't listening. "I bet you don't want me to go so that I can go back to sleep," she teased.

"You're about to win big, Kel." His feathery light touch trailed down her hip.

She giggled until his mouth met hers, and then she was lost.

A few hours later, she eased out of the bed, careful not to disturb him. They'd played for an hour before drifting off again. She was one, long, happy ache. She'd never understood what it meant to hurt so good before.

Forcing her gaze away from the sleeping, sexy marine, she pulled on her tank top and a pair of cutoffs. Rafe shifted and she paused, worried her movements might wake him. More than anything, she wanted to slip under the covers and into the warmth of his arms. Safe and adored. That was how he made her feel.

She took a step toward the bed but stopped.

No. See to Mom and Dad first.

Blast being a dutiful daughter. She tiptoed into the bathroom and washed up quietly. After brushing her teeth and pulling her hair up into a ponytail, she snuck back through the bedroom.

She checked on him one more time. Her heart squeezed at his relaxed pose. *Go before you give in to temptation.* She rushed out the door, closing it as silently as she could.

When she rounded the corner into the resort's main living room, she stopped to open a shutter and have a look at the rain. It was coming down in sheets.

She closed the shutter and, bracing herself, dashed up the stairs.

But she'd only taken a few steps when she froze. Her mother and father were on the stairs, naked, entwined in each other's arms.

"What are you doing?" she blurted, and clapped a hand over her eyes.

Never in her life would she be able to get that image out of her mind.

She shivered.

"What are *you* doing?" Her mother echoed the question, but with a great deal more amusement.

"Making sure you two hadn't done each other in," she answered, "but obviously that is not the problem."

Clothing rustled behind her. "Please just go upstairs.

I gave you separate rooms. Surely you could use *one* of those. Anybody—the staff—could have come across you. And I have a boatload of guests arriving later tonight if the storm lets up. You can't do…that sort of thing wherever you feel like it. Ugh."

Her parents' make-up sex on the staircase wasn't exactly the kind of reputation she wanted for Last Resort.

At least she would be the only one with the wounded psyche.

"It's safe, darling. You can look now." Her mother's humor only added another layer to the bizarre.

Peeking through her fingers, she took a quick peek.

Her father stood, wearing his dress slacks and her mother had her robe in place. Her hair was artfully mussed and her lips bore no trace of lipstick.

Wow.

"As you can see, we are perfectly fine." Her father cleared his throat.

"Clearly." Her hand dropped. She stared at them in wonder.

"Oh, hush. You're hardly a child and I'm guessing since your father found you so chummy with that delicious marine that you were not alone yourself last night." Raina combed her fingers through her hair, mussing it more artfully if that were possible.

"Mom!"

Her dad's low laugh started in his belly and grew louder. His shoulders shook. "Yes, I suppose I did catch them, so turnabout is fair play."

"Dad!"

What was she going to do with them?

Her father continued anyway. "Kelly, I'm fairly certain I explained to you that the marine needed to rest.

And that he shouldn't put any undue pressure on his leg."

"I am not having this conversation with you. It's none of your business, and I'd appreciate it if you would keep your business behind closed doors."

"Carter, for a surfer girl, she's kind of a prude." Her mother swept down the stairs, regal in her thick white robe. Kelly's legs refused to budge and her mother pulled her in for a hug.

"Your father and I want to apologize. You were absolutely right last night. We are two adults and we do know better." Her mother tugged at Kelly's ponytail. "I'm sorry we ruined dinner with your young man. I promise if you ever let us eat with him again, we'll behave."

"We promise," her father agreed, joining in a group hug. He pressed a kiss to Kelly's forehead. "Given everything he's done for me, the least I can do is be a little nicer to him. He seems a solid sort, not like the kind you usually date. He does have that going for him."

"Oh, Carter. That's so sweet. Silly. But sweet." Her mother leaned up and kissed him. As if by mutual consent they released Kelly and wrapped their arms around one other.

"Hey. Still standing right here." She shook her head, unable to get over their transformation from drama king and queen to teenage make-out session. She really didn't know which one was worse.

They broke their kiss but rubbed noses in a disgustingly cute gesture. Her father gazed down at her mother with such loving adoration and she returned the same to him.

Okay, Kelly liked that part. It was good to see her

parents enjoying their togetherness—but she never really needed to see them that *together* again.

"All right, darling. We'll go upstairs." Her mother pouted as if they were being punished for being in love.

"Great. I'm going to check on Rafe."

There just wasn't enough brain bleach in the world to wash away that image of her parents. Better to simply not think about it.

"She's a wonderful daughter, Raina. So much like you." Carter leaned down and kissed her again. At the first hint of another kiss and then another, Kelly bolted. She made it to the kitchen in record time. Grabbing some orange juice and a couple of glasses, she put them on a tray with some fruit and powdered beignets Adrien had made the day before. She glanced at the shutters and the strong glass they protected. "So far so good," she said to herself.

The sea must be tumultuous, she thought. If it wasn't for the rain coming down so hard and the lightning, she'd be out on the water riding the seven-foot waves. But it wasn't safe, and she had other plans.

Back in her bedroom, she found Rafe just as she had left him. Drinking in the sight of him was like a cure-all for the crazy, including her parents and their crazy fights, crazy love and being crazy about each other.

After putting the tray down on a table, she pushed the button to automatically open the shutters. It was still dark enough outside that the light didn't bother Rafe.

Her phone buzzed on the nightstand and she rushed to get it before it woke her favorite marine. Snatching it up, she darted for the bathroom. Greg's face popped up on the screen and she wrinkled her nose.

Nope. Not today.

Thumbing Decline, she turned her phone off. Her parents were upstairs. Rafe was in her bedroom. She really didn't need—or want—any more interruptions in the day.

Greg could wait.

Turning on the hot water, she stepped into the shower. As she rinsed the conditioner out of her hair, the shower door opened.

Rafe stood there, gloriously naked. She leaned over for a good-morning kiss.

"All done?" he asked with a chuckle and only a mild amount of disappointment in his voice.

"Hmm. Nope."

Nudging her aside, he stepped into the shower with her. He found the shampoo and squeezed some into his palm. "Everything okay outside?"

"So far. Just a lot of rain and noise."

He showered so much more efficiently than she did. His hair was scrubbed and rinsed in under a minute. She loved watching him. Every move was so precise.

"Anything we need to do? Family members to separate? No chefs to play guitar for? No Pilates to teach?"

"Nope." She shook her head slowly.

"Nothing for the rest of the day?"

"Not until the new guests arrive tonight. It's raining," she said coyly. "So you know what that means?"

He grinned. "What?"

"We have to play inside games." She turned all the jets on in the shower.

Rafe pressed her against the wall.

"I really like inside games," he said as his lips met hers.

Me, too.

16

SATURDAY MORNING DAWNED with a blissfully perfect blue sky and strong, steady waves. Rafe sat on the beach, enjoying the cool breeze and warm sunshine. Fijians and tourists alike spilled out in noisy ones and twos up and down the beach. Rafe learned that the surf meet had brought in more than ninety-six surfers from around the world and six wild cards. Placards and signs with names like Logi, Bryson and Smith meant little to Rafe, but he wasn't remotely surprised to see a Kelly Callahan banner.

Luckily the beaches were washed clean and smooth. Very little debris remained on the pristine sand, cluttered now by a profusion of surfboards, umbrellas and surfers who could double as swimsuit models. It was as if the storm hadn't happened. The swells and peaks were farther from the shore than he liked. He leaned forward, elbows resting on his knees, when he saw Kelly's pink board cut left and then she was on her feet, riding the huge wave.

It never failed to take his breath away. When she'd bounced out of bed and into her bikini that morning, she'd vibrated with energy. Her bright eyes danced with suppressed laughter and she dashed back and forth, warming up, stretching out and surprising him with kisses at every turn. He'd quickly gotten himself ready and followed her out to the beach.

For three blissful days, they'd made love, shared meals, and he'd watched her practice. The practice left him torn between awe and terror. She could execute aerial maneuvers, cutting off the top of the wave and coming back in. The first tube ride she took he was up and on his feet and at the water's edge without realizing he'd moved.

She wasn't just a good surfer. She was a stunning athlete. She rode the waves as if she owned them. He rather enjoyed the fact that avoiding her parents meant she stayed in his bungalow. Every night they sprawled on the sand and talked for hours. Lots of things he liked to do with women, but just talking hadn't been high on his list.

Before Kelly.

Everything seemed to come down to that term. Before Kelly. The first heats were due to start in an hour. A lot of surfers were out on the waves, like Kelly, warming up. He checked the pack of supplies she'd insisted on bringing, including fresh wax and her wax comb.

As she came into the shallow water, her expression radiated triumph and he jerked his thumb up. She waded in toward him, board tucked securely under her arm. The satisfied smile on her face couldn't have been more deserved.

He pulled a bottle of water out of the cooler and unscrewed the cap for her. When he looked up, she was standing on the shore.

Talking to Greg.

His gaze narrowed, but he waited. Greg was her manager and ex. Emphasis on the *ex*. He was probably giving her tips on her performance—not that she needed any. Or maybe he was confirming her schedule. Rafe's toes flexed against the sand. It took real effort to stay put and not walk down there to hear what they were discussing.

Greg shifted to the left, revealing Kelly's furious expression. *The hell with waiting.*

Long strides carried him toward her, but Greg took off at a lazy jog before Rafe could get there, leaving Kelly to stare after the jerk.

"Hey." Rafe touched her arm. "Everything okay?"

"Great." It sounded anything but.

"What did he do?" He tossed a look after Greg. He wasn't far enough away that even with his bum leg Rafe couldn't catch him and drag him back for an apology if need be.

"Doesn't matter." Kelly didn't quite look at him as she began to make her way over to their spot. The smile had vanished from her face and her shoulders were slumped forward.

"Kelly, babe?" He fell into step beside her. "How many pieces do you want his leg broken into?"

She shook her head and the streak of tears on her cheeks left him incensed. Just what had Greg said to her?

"I should have expected it." Her hands shook as she set the end of her board into the sand. She dashed a towel against her face, scrubbing away the evidence of her tears.

"Expected what?" He kept his words quiet and direct. He needed clear intel so he could handle the situation.

"Greg quit. He's representing Jaci Smith now. She's ranked number three, a real contender and her career is going places." Her voice cracked in the middle. "And it's stupid to be upset about it. I mean Greg and I, we weren't really working together. I'm not as invested as he wants me to be and I won't let him sell Last Resort or lock me up in contracts. And he's been calling for the last few days to tell me, but I wouldn't answer his calls. He wanted to be fair and let me know as soon as possible, but his timing sucks. Now he tells me?"

She paused, hands on her hips.

"Basically, I refused to do what he thinks is best, so he dumped me for some chick who fauns all over him. I've got to go grab my number and sign in because Greg didn't do it."

Kelly took off before he could say a word. He clenched his fists. The jerk could have dropped this news on her after the meet, or even in the three days prior he could have come by the resort or found another way to contact her. He'd had no problem showing up here before.

No, he'd waited until she had to compete.

Bastard.

Rafe would make it right. No one messed with his Kelly.

AFTER FILLING OUT her paperwork, Kelly checked in with the coordinators. Driving the negativity of the past twenty minutes out of her mind, she forced herself to focus. Greg had done this on purpose to throw her off balance. But his mind games no longer worked on her. She had Rafe. Her rock. And nothing else mattered.

She accepted her number with a wan smile and headed back to her board. She would be in the second heat. She preferred the third or fourth. That gave her time to watch the waves. The storm should have gentled the waters, but another squall a few hundred miles out was creating super peaks and swells.

Even the most experienced surfers were cautious about these dangerous waves, but Kelly craved them.

The feeling of power as she rode the tube. The adrenaline rush of coming out the other side alive. It wasn't so much about the competition as it was the moment. All that other stuff didn't really matter.

For the past couple of years, she'd forgotten that. The joy of the sport. But she was back. Today, she didn't care about the business side or what might happen if she won. She just wanted to hit some good waves.

Rafe waited for her by her board and he took the number out of her hand, replacing it with a bottle of water. "Drink."

She tipped back the bottle obediently while he taped the waterproof number to her back. She wasn't sure she would ever get used to the way his touch sent her body into hyperdrive. Every time his fingers glided over her skin, he left a small tingle.

"Thanks."

"You're gonna win, babe." He held her face in his hands and the utter faith in his blue eyes took her breath away. He leaned in and kissed her hard. "Forget him."

She laughed through the wobbly feeling. "Who?" She winked.

"Good. These waves are nothing compared to what

you were riding the other day. And it isn't about the winning. Today we're just having fun. No matter what happens, we will celebrate tonight." He gave her a mischievous grin. "Though, that might be just as much for me as it is for you."

She smiled and then scanned the beach; the first heat was lining up. They would paddle out, match the wave speed and pop up for the ride.

The judges didn't score on mistakes, only on successes. Where the surfer rode the wave, what maneuvers they performed, and their professionalism at not wave-hopping to steal from another surfer.

It took timing, precision and a deep understanding of just how tempestuous a mistress the ocean was. Her gaze skimmed the horizon. The waves were coming in a lot faster than only an hour ago.

Rafe's arm was wrapped loosely around her waist, but he let her concentrate. She snuck a glance at him from the corner of her eye. He really was a great guy like that. She explained the competition to him during a long, lazy soak in the tub during the storm. How she liked to measure the speed, calculate the best moves and how she knew when to pop.

Several riders in the first heat wiped out and she winced in sympathy for them. It was easy to see why they were in a rush. These waves were massive, and it took them a bit to build speed. One of the surfers made it through most of the tube when her board popped, without her on it.

The patrol was out in a flash searching for her. And it took a few minutes before they hauled her from the water and onto the beach.

Watching her limp through the sand, Kelly suppressed a cringe. A couple of lifeguards in red vests guided her to the first-aid tent.

"Hang ten?" Rafe gave her a small, questioning smile and a quick squeeze.

She didn't have the heart to tell him what "hang ten" really meant. There was no way she'd be hanging her toes off the end of her board on purpose. "At least five." She feigned the confidence she was lacking. If he knew, he'd worry and she didn't want that. Grabbing her board, she headed down to the water with the others in her heat.

Including Jaci Smith.

Her spine stiffened at the sight of the redhead's profile.

She paddled after her, keeping an eye on where the redhead pointed her board. Halfway to the break, she realized she'd forgotten to time the waves.

Stupid. Stupid. Stupid. Get your head together.

But it was too late, the waves were rolling in so fast that foamy whitecaps appeared ahead of them and she had to turn, or risk cutting into someone else's wave. Her gut churned. She'd no sooner twisted and popped than she felt the pull in the wave.

The back of her board slapped upward and caught her across the jaw and she plowed under. Only years of experience brought her back up to the surface of the water. She caught her board and rolled onto it, body riding in to the shallows coughing and spluttering.

Rafe caught her hand and straightened her board, but he didn't try to take either when she walked out of the knee-deep water. She didn't know what made her want to cry more—that he had enough faith in her to let her stand on her own two feet or that she had just wiped out in front of her peers and proved Greg's point for him. Her career was quite possibly over.

"Water" was all Rafe said as he pointed her back to the towels and umbrella. He yanked open the cooler and wrapped some ice in a towel and then pressed it to her right cheek. She frowned.

"How bad is it?"

"Gonna be a hell of a beauty mark." He squinted at her. "How's the head?"

"Fine. I just smacked myself in the face, like an idiot, a washed-up, doesn't-know-when-she's-done idiot." The same idiot that used her sister's name to land a great boyfriend. Guilt piled on top of her already shaky confidence and she wanted to collapse. She didn't *need* to compete anymore.

Why am I even here?

"Listen, stop with the negativity. Shake it off. Three-fourths of the surfers have wiped out on these waves and…" He dragged out his words, obviously uncertain. "Just plowed under."

He was trying to talk her language. It was so sweet.

He slanted a hand across his forehead, shielding his eyes. "What is up with the water?"

"Storm moving in…brings stronger waves. They're extremely fast, and there's a tight pull that, if you don't watch out, will land you on your ass." Which she knew very well before she swam out there, trying to prove something.

"You're going to have to teach me how you see that." Holding the ice pack to her face, she downed another swallow of water and stepped closer to him.

"Look out past the point where you see the surfer turning. See the ripples on top of the water? They take

time to build up speed and form the wave, but you can
see how fast they're moving by judging where the break
is and the crest begins to form. The perfect wave is the
one you get right in front of. You have all the momentum and none of the backlash. Trick is, you have to
time it perfectly." *You have to feel the water and know
when it's ready.*

The fourth heat was already on the move, paddling
out toward the break.

"It's closer in this time, isn't it?"

"Yeah." Her heart rate calmed as she breathed deep.
It was a lot closer. It was moving in five- to ten-foot
increments.

The break jumped again as she watched, catching
four paddlers and dumping them before they could pop.
"That's a tropical storm."

She could kick herself. She canted her gaze across
the water. "It was listed as a depression this morning
at five, but it's probably been upgraded."

"What do you need?"

"An accurate weather forecast." She glanced at her
watch. Rafe wasn't kidding. Most of the fourth heat had
wiped out. A hum of noise rose up around the judges'
table and runners jogged out to assist the surfers.

"You're up for the seventh heat, Callahan!" someone called out.

The judges weren't bothering to write the scores on
the boards with this many wipeouts. Her jaw clenched.
Then Rafe turned his phone to her with a look of triumph.

"Tropical storm. Upgraded ninety minutes ago. It's
moving northwest at thirty knots. What else you need?"

The gain in wind force would continue to increase

the wave speed. If she were off, even a little, she'd fail again. "I can't do this."

"Yes. You can." Rafe crowded in front of her, blocking her view of the waves. "Look at me."

Her gaze crashed into his.

"Kelly, you were born for this. Every bit of you is a true surfer. I've never seen anyone glide through the water like you do. You were talking about how good some of these people are, but none of them rode waves like you did the other day. You know the water. Forget everything else. This is *your* beach. You go show all these tourists how it's done." No hesitation marked his words and he left no room for doubt.

The sixth heat ran into the ocean with their boards.

"Someone told me once that all you have to do is believe, everything else is just the work. I believe in you, you can make this work." Rafe's encouragement echoed the letter she had written to him soon after he began his physical therapy. He'd told her about the pain and the frustration. A costly admission for a marine. And now those were the exact words he was giving to her.

He said he believed in her.

She believed in him.

"Okay." She closed her eyes and filled her lungs with sea air. She could do this. "You ready to see me fly?"

"Ooh-rah."

She laughed, a fresh burst of sound that relaxed the steel grip of fear attacking her chest. Grabbing her board, she jogged over to the water.

Moments later, after paddling out to sea, she sat up on her board and watched each wave carefully, her gaze locked on the break.

The thrum of the crowd, the music, the scent of burg-

ers and beer—they all faded. She increased her speed
as the break shifted, inching inland. The wind against
her face pushed back the damp tendrils.

The roar of the water filled her with raw energy. Taking a deep breath, she caught the front of the wave and
she exploded on top of the board. A spin, a hop, and a
flip and she crested the wave as it started to tunnel and
her heart soared.

She flew.

17

RAFE HELD HIS breath. His hands were clenched at his sides as he watched Kelly paddle toward a massive wave. She turned, catching the wave, and he hollered and held his fists aloft.

She couldn't hear him cheer, but it didn't matter.

As he watched through the binoculars the look on her face told him everything he needed to know.

She owned that wave.

Pure joy lit up her face as she swam back to shore. She walked with pride and he couldn't wait to kiss her. He thought she'd rejoin him, but the judges directed her back into the shallows. She'd made the cut for the next set of heats. Or whatever they called them.

"If she spent as much time on her surfing as she does on that resort, she could own this circuit." Greg stood next to him, pressed jeans, white polo shirt flapping in the breeze. His sunglasses hid his eyes and his hands were in his pockets.

"She could own anything she wanted to. She doesn't have to prove that to anyone, especially to you." Rafe counseled himself on patience. He was here for Kelly, not to pound her ex into the sand. Still, the latter did hold a wild kind of appeal.

"Hey, calling it like I see it, man. Remember, she doesn't like to be told what to do, even when it's in her best interest. She'll jump ship when she gets bored. You won't know what hit you."

Was he really talking about Kelly? Did he even know the woman he'd once represented and supposedly dated? "Thanks for the advice, but I think I'll do us both a favor and ignore it. Didn't seem to work for you with Kelly—she's moving on to bigger and better things."

"Excuse me?" Greg took a firm step toward him.

Rafe smiled ever so slightly. "You heard me. Only a coward wanting to sabotage someone decides to strike right before the person has to compete. Just because you can't do the job doesn't mean you get to tear down the woman who can. She's better off without you."

"She'd be a nobody without me, G.I. Schmo. I made her Kelly Callahan. She wouldn't have had a single gig without me because she was too busy surfing to worry about the real work." Greg took another step toward him. "She owes me. And not even a dumb jock like you can change that."

What did she ever see in this joker?

A woman wearing a familiar sportswear logo jogged toward them. It took Rafe a moment, but he remembered the spokesmodel deal Kelly had mentioned.

Rafe grinned. "Uh, Greg…"

The man had to be bottling up a lot of frustration, because he telegraphed his right hook louder than a mess hall call. Rafe could have avoided it. He could have caught Greg's fist and broken his hand. He could have twisted and slammed him into the sand.

But he did none of those things.

Instead, he took it right on the jaw.

The hit barely rocked him, but he jerked his head to the side all the same. The smart-looking woman in the Baywear polo let out an audible gasp.

"Mr. Sanders!"

Greg spun around and the wide-eyed shock on his face was priceless. "This isn't at all what it looks like," Greg pleaded. "It's just a disagreement between men."

"What I know, Mr. Sanders," she said through tight lips, "is that you punched this man. That is not the kind of behavior Baywear wants to be associated with, no matter what your disagreement might have been."

"You planned this," Greg spit out, whirling back toward Rafe. The woman gave him a wide berth, shaking her head.

Rafe had been right. The woman was with Baywear. He rubbed his chin, playing up his part. "You might want to consider some anger management classes *man,* you're really harshing the buzz." He'd learned that phrase from Kelly when he wanted her to rest for a bit rather than keep training, and she'd wink and tell him that he was harshing her buzz.

Taking a hit to reveal Greg's true colors, not to mention the guy who'd tried to ruin Kelly's performance today, was the least he could do. Well, the least he could do and still let the other man walk away with his limbs intact. Hitting him in the wallet was Rafe's best blow.

"We're done, Mr. Sanders. Consider the offer for Jaci's contract withdrawn. Baywear prefers professional behavior from all parties involved." The woman brushed him off and held out her hand to Rafe. "Amanda Clark, Mr.…?"

"McCawley." Rafe gave the offered hand a quick squeeze. "But you can call me Rafe."

"Thank you. Who do you represent?" Her gaze swept him from head to toe. He could almost see the wheels turning in her assessment.

"My girlfriend," he replied, searching the surfers for Kelly's suit, and his heart stopped. She was paddling toward another turbulent wave, rising up on the swell and popping to her feet. "Out there."

The muscles in Rafe's leg clenched painfully. The wave was a monster and she did a pirouette at the top, the entire board spinning up into the air with her. She came down on top of the water, riding the surface like satin.

The pure terror clawing up his throat was worse than the snakes. Worse than the bullets that had ripped his flesh. It was Kelly against nature. Only she didn't fight the wave, she harnessed it. Claimed it as her ride.

Magnificent.

The pride welled up in him as she coasted along. Damn, the woman could do anything. Even men twice her size hadn't been able to hold a wave like that one.

He would do anything for her—even support her in a sport where she risked her life. He'd never thought of it until now, but he knew she'd burrowed her way into his soul and staked her claim on him the same way she had that wave.

His lungs begged for oxygen and so he sucked in a breath as she made it onto the beach. A roar of delight came up from the crowd and he quickly looked to the judges.

"All tens. Fantastic. You know, Kelly Callahan is who

we wanted first as our spokesmodel. I had thought that Sanders represented her…"

"He did, Ms. Clark." Only years of discipline kept his voice calm even as he wanted to cheer along with the crowd at Kelly's success. "That relationship was terminated earlier today. I'm helping Kelly out temporarily," Rafe said. And he would until they found the right manager for her career. *They.* As if she needed his help. His surfer girl had proved she could handle anything that came her way.

Greg shot him a murderous look. The man loitered close enough to overhear the conversation and didn't miss Rafe's implication that Kelly had been the one to end their business arrangement.

"Excellent. We are a little pressed for time on the decision, but here's my card. We can give you one week to decide. Please let Kelly know that we want her and we're willing to negotiate a very favorable contract."

"I'll do that." He accepted her card and offered his genuine thanks, but then he quickly jogged over to meet Kelly, Baywear and Greg already forgotten. He had to touch her.

Kelly threw her arms about his neck, wet and wiggling with excitement. Catching her, he swung her around and kissed her hard. "You rocked that wave."

"Yeah, I did." She peppered his face with kisses. "And I couldn't have done it without you."

"WELL, I THINK that went a lot better than last time."

It was after dinner and Kelly and Rafe were strolling along the beach. The tropical storm had bypassed the island and left a gorgeous sunset in its wake.

"I'm not sure your dad actually ate anything." Rafe

grinned from ear to ear. "He was too busy admiring your mom."

Kelly laughed. "I saw that. She was busy doing it right back to him, though. It is kind of weird, but I'm hopeful that maybe they've figured some things out finally."

Rafe joined his hand with hers and they swung them together. The moment seemed like a picture postcard. The warm sand tickled her toes and she laid her head against Rafe's shoulder.

"For your sake and theirs," he said, "I hope so. At least tonight it was steak and potatoes, I definitely approve of that meal."

Seagulls rose up, wings fluttering, and they darted farther along the beach.

"They're happy. Dad didn't buy Mom anything and she didn't demand that they race back home for some party. In fact, I heard them talking about taking a cruise. Dad had this sort of tetchy look and then Mom said it was a golf cruise." More laughter bubbled up inside her.

"I'm sorry you didn't win today." He squeezed her hand and she danced forward until he tugged her back.

"I'm not. I probably would have given up if you hadn't been there, and I would have missed one of the best waves of my career. And I scored the only tens of the day, so second looks pretty damn sweet. That Jaci didn't make the top ten has nothing to do with how happy I am right now." It was mean and shallow, but Greg's expression had been priceless.

"Speaking of which, I talked to an Amanda Clarke from Baywear. She said they really want you." Rafe waggled his brows playfully. He let go of her hand and slung his arm around her shoulder.

"What?" Blinking, she reached up to push a misbehaving strand of hair out of her eyes. "I assumed that deal was sunk after Greg dumped me."

"Hmm. Maybe not."

And there it was—that mischievous grin she loved so much. "What did you do?"

"Nothing. But the rumor is *you* dumped Greg, not the other way around. Seems that Baywear *really* sees you as their spokesmodel. You said that was something you wanted to do, and they've given you a week to think about that big contract."

Rafe couldn't understand just how tempting that apple was to her. Or had been. She wasn't quite so sure that was what she wanted anymore.

Greg was right about one thing. While she did love Last Resort, she missed surfing competitively with her friends. Today had reminded her of why she wanted to surf in the first place.

She loved it.

Could she manage the resort and compete?

And where would that leave her with Rafe?

"I know. But it's a lot to figure out. The contract would be for a year or more. And I have to compete in a certain amount of meets each year."

"Then negotiate for the time you are willing to give Baywear. I can help you with that. I happen to have a way with people." He smiled. "Besides, I've got some tough decisions to make about what I want to do next. Maybe we can help each other out."

Shock bolted through her. "What are you talking about?"

"I thought I was a career marine, but maybe there's something I'm meant to do that doesn't involve the corps. I'm healing, but it's slow going and I have a feeling this hip will always be a problem for me."

"You're still early in the recovery process, Rafe. We need to get you back into yoga and Pilates. We can build your strength and flexibility." She didn't want him to give up. He'd come so far.

"Sure and we can do that. But it's hard to do yoga with you if who knows where we are."

The speculation in his voice confused her. *What is he saying?* She tried to sort through her emotions. "I have saltwater brain. I don't understand what you mean."

"Hey, I've got a business degree, I'm good with money. You need a manager who has your best interests at heart and looks after you. I guess I'm applying for the job."

Kelly frowned. Applying for the job? He wanted to be her manager? He wanted to stick around. But did he want her, or was it her career he was interested in?

"You're overthinking, Kelly." His murmur tickled her ear. She stopped, tipping her head up to look at him.

"Why?"

"Why what?" He met her gaze evenly, a hint of a smile flirting around his wonderful lips.

"Why do you want to be my manager? I mean—it's flattering that you'd consider it and I love that you want to—" This wasn't coming out right.

"There will be a learning curve, but I'm up for the challenge. And I could assist you with this place if you need it, although you seem to handle it just fine. Don't you trust me?"

Did she trust him?

"Yes." No hesitation, no retreat, she reminded herself. "What I don't want—"

He stopped and faced her, his expression intense. "What don't you want, Kelly?"

"I don't want to be only business partners. Call me demanding, but I can hire anyone to be my manager. Okay, well, not anyone, but you're my—" What was he? Was he a boyfriend? Her lover? What title did he have?

"Yes, I am yours. And as they say in business, we can definitely negotiate satisfying terms."

He was teasing her. "Mean."

He quickly leaned in and captured her lips in a long, slow, toe-curling kiss. His tongue stroked hers and his hands gently caressed her back and slid down to her hips. She had no idea how long they stood there, just wrapped around each other—kissing.

But, damn, the man knew how to kiss.

After several moments, he broke the embrace and looked at her. "I do want to be your manager and I stand by that offer. But I'm a greedy man, Kelly. I'm going to want a lot more than just your business interests."

A slow smile spread across her face. "Let's negotiate."

SHE COULD GET used to waking up to the pleasant ache in her limbs. Stretching her arms out, Kelly inhaled the breeze blowing gently through the windows and the rich aroma of freshly brewed coffee. The only thing missing was Rafe. Sitting up, she saw the folded piece of paper on his pillow: "Gone to town. Be back by lunch. Save me a wave. R."

She buried her face in his pillow and reveled in the distinct, masculine scent of him. Okay, so she had to wait until lunch to see him. With so many guests, she had a great deal to accomplish before he returned. One glance at the clock and she was up and running.

Four hours to tackle her to-do list and then she could spend time with her man, Rafe. She was still grinning when she let herself out of the bungalow and strode toward the resort. She braided her damp hair back from her face. The bruise on her cheek was still a bit dark, but with almost no swelling she barely noticed it.

Rafe wanted to act as her business manager. They'd talked about it late into the night. He loved this place and didn't see any reason she needed to get rid of it. In fact, he suggested she hire an assistant to shoulder the work when she was off the island and an accountant to do the books. Both would free up a lot of her time. Plenty of her employees were up for the assistant job. She considered Adrien right away and Rafe seconded the idea.

But what she loved most about Rafe was that he wanted her to make the plan and let him worry about how to execute it. They even made up a wish list of terms for her Baywear contract. Whenever she hesitated on an item, he told her to add it.

Reach for exactly what you want, worry about the details later. The worst they'll say is no. But if we don't ask for it, we can't get it. His words echoed in her mind. His words and the way he said *we.* They were a *we,* an *us,* a *team,* and, yes, it had only been a short time and there were a lot of details to work out.

But she'd waited her entire life for someone to look at her the way Rafe did. Nothing could puncture the sunshine of her morning. She even whistled.

"Good morning, sweetheart!" Her mother's enthusiastic greeting halted her footsteps and Kelly covered her eyes, just in case.

Her dad's chuckle made her feel a little better. "We're perfectly decent."

And they were, sitting out on the veranda with a pair of drinks. Their casual dress and her mother's apparent lack of cosmetic enhancement gave Kelly pause. "Good morning."

"Congratulations. You were fabulous yesterday." Her mother blew her a kiss.

"You saw me?" Kelly blinked. That was a first. In all her years of competition, she couldn't recall a single one where her mother congratulated her personally. Oh, she always sent flowers, and even had a charm bracelet made with a dozen different charms celebrating her surfing victories—but this was a first.

"Yes, I did. Your father and I were there first thing in the morning. We saw everything. Including how your Rafe got one over on George."

"Greg, mom. And what are you talking about?"

"I told you he wouldn't tell her." Carter beamed. "No man likes to brag about how he protects his woman."

Kelly walked up the steps slowly and leaned a hip against the railing. "What are you two talking about?"

"Well, it seems there is a rumor that Glen was negotiating a certain Baywear deal for several million dollars but lost it when he completely embarrassed himself by trying to punch out his ex-girlfriend's new manager after she fired him for incompetence." Her mother seemed almost giddy with the news.

What did a person say to that? Kelly didn't even realize there'd been a scuffle. In fact, she hadn't seen any mark on Rafe at all.

"It's so romantic." Her mother sighed and propped her chin on her hand. "Would you let someone punch you for me, darling?"

Her father looked thoughtful and glanced down at his hands. "There was a time when I would have needed these to be in perfect condition, but now I will happily do the punching if need be."

Raina cooed and Kelly couldn't help but laugh. "I am going to guess that things are better between the two of you?"

"Yes, they are. And that's all we're going to tell you. We promise to not involve our children in our issues anymore." Raina beamed as Carter lifted her hand to his lips for a kiss.

"Back to you, Kelly, because your mother is right. You were fantastic out there on the waves. The next time you have a competition, you let us know, we'll make a special trip to see it."

Kelly welled up—she couldn't fight the emotion. Pride shone in her mother's eyes and respect in her father's. Until that moment she hadn't realized how much she truly needed their approval.

She'd always known they loved and supported her. Their dysfunctional communication aside, they were her parents. Love like that doesn't just disappear, but they hadn't been demonstrative or so brazenly approving before.

"Thanks, really, both of you. I have a lot to get done. We're reopening the resort. Would you like me to reserve the honeymoon bungalow for you?"

"No, I think we're going to leave you and your young man alone while I whisk your mother away for a secret escape." Her father grinned.

"Oh!" Raina straightened up immediately. "Where?"

"If I told you, darling, it wouldn't be a secret." Carter picked up his drink and took a sip, his expression very mischievous.

"But how will I know what to pack if I don't know where we're going? What clothes should I bring?"

"Who said you'll need clothes?"

Her father's playful leer was Kelly's cue to leave. "La-la-la-la-la—daughter running away now." She plugged her fingers in her ears and hurried off. Though she couldn't resist pausing at the door to look back.

Her father had moved closer to her mother to kiss her with such tenderness. Yeah, they had their issues, but times like this told her they could work it out if they tried hard enough.

Someday, that could be her and Rafe grossing their kids out.

Not if she wasn't honest with him.

And that means it's time for you to spill your guts. No more lies. No more half-truths. No more letting it hang over your head. Tonight, you tell him and put all your cards on the table.

Rafe wanted to be her partner. He deserved nothing but the truth. He would understand.

He believed in her. She would believe in him.

18

RAFE THANKED THE cab driver and passed him a tip before sliding out of the backseat. The trip to town had taken longer than he'd expected. He had planned a lunchtime return and now here it was after two. Still, he was satisfied.

The orchids and roses he'd chosen at the flower shop to apologize for his tardiness were pretty and fragrant. The resort bustled. Open windows on every floor let in the swift ocean breeze. He saw a maid carrying towels down to the bungalows while a gardener tidied the lush green lawn. The gardener noticed Rafe and threw him a friendly wave.

Guests must have arrived, but everyone seemed to be keeping to themselves. Kelly had been right about that. The guests wanted privacy and a haven away from their public lives.

He couldn't blame them.

His bungalow had become his and Kelly's hideaway from the main house and he wouldn't mind it if they moved in there permanently—or had a larger one built away from the resort so she always had a private escape.

The porch was empty and so were the salon and the dining room. He wandered through the rest of the first floor, checking for her, before he stuck his hand in his pocket for his cell phone. Then he heard her voice.

Tracking it like a beacon, he dodged a valet pulling a huge trunk toward the staircase and slid right up behind Kelly, where she was relaxing against the kitchen door frame. "We should stick with the buffet breakfasts this week, right? They're always popular and with the increased traffic to the island, thanks to the competition, we can offer them as an enticing alternative to what the other hotels have. Maybe we'll get some extra business."

Adrien noticed him immediately, but Kelly kept talking. "What about adding a few more rounds of surfing lessons? I can do the ones in the morning, but if we bring in an afternoon and evening instructor…"

Rafe's arm snaked around her middle and he tugged her backward. "You would have more free time for me."

She yelped and the papers in her hand fluttered to the floor. Amusement lit up her face. At the sight of the flowers, she gasped.

"It occurred to me that a beautiful woman deserves beautiful things and I didn't have flowers for you after the competition, so let's agree that these are serving double duty."

"Are they, now?" She looked at him skeptically, a playful glint in her eyes.

"Yes, they're my you're-beautiful-and-talented-and-I'm-sorry-I-missed-lunch flowers." He spread his hands over her hips, loving the way she fit against him. His gaze swept over her sweat-dampened face and the dirt smudges tracking across her brow and one cheek.

"What?" she asked, giving him a quick, fierce hug.

"You're pretty when you're all mussed up." He waggled his eyebrows and she giggled.

"Let me put these in water."

He caught her arm as she started to walk away. "Actually, Adrien will probably be nice and put those in water for us. Right now I need to steal the boss lady."

They skirted more of the cleaning crew on their way out toward the front entrance. "Rafe!" Kelly tugged on his arm as they started down the steps. "You're not limping."

He glanced at his leg and shrugged. "It's sore, but loose. Don't need to limp when I have such a great yoga and Pilates instructor around." He urged her down the rest of the steps and paused at the driveway.

The place where they'd first met.

He turned then to face her. His business in town had taken a lot longer than he'd expected it to. The longest part was getting his friend Will on the phone and his new C.O. Both men supported Rafe's decision to accept an honorable discharge. He'd have to return to the States in a couple of weeks to sign his release papers, but he wanted to take Kelly with him.

"Listen, Kelly, I got you a present…."

Her eyes widened, but he held up a finger to stave off any questions.

"Before you say anything, know that this is not because you placed second in the competition or received an awesome contract offer and not because you run a resort that I never want to leave, but because you're you."

Reaching into his pocket, he pulled out a silver surfboard hanging on a silver chain. It was attached to one of his dog tags. Her lips parted and she let out a soft sigh that went straight to his heart. He placed the delicate piece in her upturned palm.

"Surfer girl, you own my heart."

Tears dampened her eyes and he chuckled, catching one as it splashed down onto her cheek.

"No crying. You helped put this marine back together and I'm yours. If you'll have me." Probably not the most polished of proposals, but he wasn't making plans to go anywhere else except right here. "And if you can't answer me today, that's all right. I'll be here every day until you can. And we don't have to talk marriage yet, but—"

"I'm all for it." Holding the chain carefully between her fingers, Kelly bit her lip. "I love it, but before we make any decisions, there's something I need to tell you. It's kind of funny and more than a little embarrassing, but..."

A car pulling into the driveway interrupted them. Kelly squinted past him and he had fully intended to ignore what was happening, until she went pale. Casting a glance over his shoulder, Rafe wanted to swear.

Mimi.

The drop-dead gorgeous model—all five-feet-eleven of her, with porcelain skin, charcoal-black lashes and pure black hair that fell like liquid velvet—squealed. She whooped like a teen and dropped all elegant pretenses to race around the cab to throw her arms around Kelly.

KELLY COULDN'T BELIEVE IT.

She returned her sister's enthusiastic hug and closed her fist around the surfboard and dog tag necklace to keep from dropping it. Rafe backed up a step, his expression tense.

"So sorry for barging in like this," Mimi said to Rafe in what was her trademark dismissive tone. "I haven't seen my sister in months. I left as soon as I got Mom's message that she had some harebrained scheme to make Dad jealous. I'm sorry I didn't get here sooner, but I had a hard time canceling my next shoot and you know Sebastian, he didn't want me to go, but I told him I just had to rescue you from Mom's nonsense."

Hurricane Mimi had officially landed.

"Hey, Mimi." Rafe's brows drew together in a frown.

Her sister flicked a look back at him, a complete lack of recognition on her face. "Hello…?"

"Rafe. Rafe McCawley." Uncertainty and unease crawled across his face. When Mimi continued to stare at him blankly, he sighed. "Don't be that way. I'm sorry it didn't work out for us, but I did try to get a hold of you after I got here."

"What are you talking about?" Now it was Mimi's turn to frown.

Kelly winced. "How about we go inside and get Mimi settled, and then we can sort this out."

Five more minutes, Mimi. Just five more minutes.

If she could separate them, she could spill her guts to Rafe about the lie. Why she ever thought not telling him when he'd arrived was a good idea, she couldn't begin to fathom. Sweat slipped down her spine and her heart raced.

"No, I want to know what he's talking about. Have we met?" Mimi put a manicured hand on her hip, her chin going up in the same stubborn manner as their mother's.

"'Have we met?'" Rafe blinked, a profusion of emotions running riot through his blue eyes before they hardened. "New York fashion show? I walked you home? We've been writing for months. Does this not ring a bell with you?"

"No." Mimi shrugged a shoulder and Kelly gritted her teeth. This couldn't get any worse.

"Mimi, darling!" Her mother's voice sliced through the tension and Kelly decided she'd discovered the social equivalent of a wipeout. She'd miscalculated the wave and now she was hanging ten off a board that was going to slam her fast and hard into the water.

"Rafe, you have to understand, Mimi's been traveling and she gets a little tired. She doesn't always know what she's saying." Her mother swooped in and embraced Mimi. Her father trailed behind her.

"Of course I know what I'm saying. Do you know how many shows I've done in New York? I've been to Paris, Milan, and Saõ Paulo all in the last three weeks. I'm sorry I don't remember you, and I certainly haven't been writing you any letters." Irritation flamed in Mimi's face, but Kelly stopped looking at her. Instead, she forced herself to meet Rafe's gaze and the anger that blazed in them.

"If you'll excuse us, I need to talk to Rafe." Kelly reached for his hand and tried not to be hurt when he didn't take it. He motioned for her to go ahead of him and she led him away from her family and her mother's hushed and hurried explanations to Mimi.

She and Rafe made for the beach in absolute silence. It wasn't until they got there that she finally had to say something. "I'm sorry."

"For what, exactly?" His ice-cold tone matched his

frigid posture. He thrust his hands in his pockets and stared at her, his sexy smile hidden.

"I lied to you. It didn't start out as a big lie, it started out as one person reaching out to another…."

Rafe exhaled slowly. "Cut to the chase, Kelly. Please." He seemed to tack the last word on as an afterthought. The warm sunshine and golden beach were a stark contrast to the darkness brewing between them.

"I wrote the letters. I pretended to be Mimi and I wrote the letters to you." Pain flickered across his expression before he shuttered it away and she rushed on. "I read the notes you sent her and they were sweet and thoughtful and caring. I think I started falling for you just in what you said to Mimi, and then you were hurt and you sounded so lonely. I had Mimi's email password and I checked it every day after that first note."

Tears clogged her throat, but she pressed on. "I wanted her to answer you, but when it didn't look like she would, I did. Then you wrote back. So I answered it and one thing led to another…"

"And you had a great time at my expense. Romancing your sister's half-forgotten and completely discarded date. What was the plan? Lead me on? Bring me out here because you felt sorry for me?" Every sentence was like a lash against her soul. She deserved it. Kelly had lied to him, but not for the reasons he listed.

"No. I liked you. In fact, I thought you were wonderful, and I wanted to get to know you better." Though it was the truth, her words sounded trite and hollow.

"Because I wrote some sappy story to your sister? Really?" It was as if he were a stranger to her now. He simply stood there, glaring. "So why didn't you tell me the truth when I got here? After I'd flown *halfway around the world* to meet a lie?"

"Because I didn't want you to go. I didn't know I would fall for you or that we would get involved. And then you left that message for Mimi…." She swallowed and Rafe's anger seemed about to boil up to the surface.

"You listened to the message?"

She couldn't lie anymore. It was all or nothing. "Yes. The number I sent you was directed to my cell phone. It wasn't Mimi's."

Rafe nodded slowly, his lips whitening into a hard line. "Well played, Miss Callahan. Well played. If you'll excuse me, I have some arrangements to make and some packing to do. Thank you for the vacation. I'm afraid you're going to have to find yourself another manager."

"Rafe, wait." She grabbed at his arm, the necklace falling down into the sand between them.

"Let go, Kelly," he said through gritted teeth.

"I need you to understand."

"I do." He spoke in a gentle tone. "I get it. You wanted attention. You wanted to feel useful. You wanted someone to need you. I can appreciate that. I was broken, and you patched me up. Thanks for that. But I don't like head games, and this is the super championship of all head games. I'll be gone before nightfall."

He strode away.

Kelly pressed a hand against her mouth, fighting the scream crawling up the back of her throat. Sound rushed in again, the call of birds, the pounding of the surf and the shattering of her heart.

IT TOOK RAFE less than ten minutes to throw his gear into his bag. It wasn't as if he'd brought that much with him. In the bathroom he grabbed his toiletries and froze at the sight of her red-and-white bikini hanging off the shower rod.

Hurt speared him, but he shuttled it aside. Everything he knew about her, everything he'd told himself since he'd arrived—her honesty, her freshness and her open attitude—seemed somehow tainted by the lie.

She saw my face when I heard Mimi wasn't here. She even tried to comfort me when I saw Mimi and her playboy boyfriend on television. What the hell was she thinking?

In the bedroom, he moved the sheets and a pair of her panties landed on the floor. His heart squeezed. She'd teased him just last night, "dressing" for dinner in lingerie only, since he suggested she skip the dress.

They'd laughed so hard.

Get a grip, man. He needed to get away from this place. Everywhere he turned, he saw some souvenir of their time together.

Hell, her pink surfboard was resting in the corner. Her bottle of nail polish sat on the table by his bed and he knew her damp dress still lay in a tangled pile with his towels in the hamper.

Grabbing his phone, he called the local airport. No one answered, but he didn't care. He had to get off the island.

I'm a damn fool. I'm sitting here mooning over a woman who lied to get me here. Of course, she hadn't lied to seduce him. Or maybe she had.

He thought he knew her. But what did he really know? She gave a great massage, surfed like the professional she was and was the most generous lover he'd ever met. Pain spiked through him again.

This was why he didn't do relationships. Never had he dated a girl more than two or three times. And he should have kept it that way.

She made him think about plans, about a future. He was ready to walk away from the Marines, retire and travel the world with her.

And she had lied. Not once, but multiple times. The truth was something that was important to him. He couldn't stand it when people lied to him. And he'd believed in her. Believed in what they could have been.

Dammit. He picked up the bag and slammed his way out of the bungalow, heading for the driveway. Even if he couldn't get a ride into town, he could be at the airport in an hour at a fast march. As much as his left leg ached, it didn't match what was happening to his heart.

Kelly stood at the end of the driveway, a cab idling behind her, her red-rimmed eyes betraying her.

"You're really going?"

"Yeah…I need some space. I'm sure there's a flight in a couple of hours."

She nodded slowly. "There's another storm coming. It might be difficult to get away."

"I'll take my chances," he said as he tried to hold his temper.

"I wish—well, never mind what I wish. I asked the driver to wait for you. I've already paid the fee. Be careful, long plane rides can't be good for the leg. Make sure you get up and walk around when you can." She held out a small bag. "This is the ointment we used on your leg."

How well he remembered those first few days when she'd used her gentle hands to ease his muscles. He'd been an aching mess when he'd arrived. She was the reason his leg hardly bothered him, why he slept so soundly and had serenity back in his life.

She's also the reason you're standing here like an open wound. Get in the cab.

"You deserve better," she said so quietly that he had to strain to hear it. "A lot better and I hope you find it. You made me believe in me again, you—you helped me believe that a person can have more than one dream and it's okay to give up or let go of the ones that don't make you happy. Thank you for that."

He wanted to sweep her into his arms and kiss away the hurt in her eyes, but she'd made him look like a fool. It was such a stupid lie, and she'd ruined what had been the best thing in his life.

He nodded and quickly climbed into the cab. As the driver put the car in gear, he could see Kelly staring after him, her tears spilling again.

Guilt assailed him. She looked so lonely and lost. *She'll be okay. She has the resort. Her parents are here. Mimi.* He grunted at the last. The driver picked up speed as they left the gravel road and bounced up onto the surfaced one.

His thigh and hip protested, but he ignored them until the driver swore and the cab squealed to a halt. Mimi was standing in front of the taxi, waving frantically at them. She circled around the cab and jumped in beside him. "You don't mind if I ride with you to the airport."

She rapped the glass and the driver grumbled, but the car started moving again.

"Can I help you?" Rafe stared at the model warily. Her failure to remember him was bad enough, but she really didn't match up to the picture he had of her in his mind. Not anymore.

Once he'd met Kelly, there wasn't another woman in the world who would compare. She was beautiful, kind…

"Nope. I did want to tell you, though, that I'm sorry for my sister. My family seems to have some real boundary issues and they don't communicate well." Her red-painted lips drew back into a practiced grimace. "But what can you do? Her heart was in the right place. She just forgets that you can't think with your heart, you know? That, and she acts so impulsively. For what it's worth, *Rafe,* I do remember you and I'm sorry I didn't answer your email. Okay? But hey, it was a fun night."

She pressed her hand to his shoulder and he shifted away from her.

He couldn't stand this a second longer—he had to defend his surfer girl. "Kelly's heart is what makes her special, Mimi. She doesn't confuse prestige and fame for genuine affection, and she doesn't treat people badly because she's in a position to do so. She bends over backward to accommodate the people she loves."

Mimi shrugged. "Being a martyr doesn't make you special, Rafe. It just makes you sad and lonely while the people you love leave and do whatever they want. Kelly would be better off if she remembered that instead of giving her heart so freely to people who will toss it aside the first time she makes a mistake."

"It was more than a mistake. She lied to me for months. And she's had plenty of opportunity here to tell me the truth."

"You know, people think I'm shallow, and they're right, except when it comes to my family. Let me tell you something, Mr. Marine. I'm sure you've never made a mistake or had a white lie turn into a mess that seemed impossible to clean up. You're probably perfect. But the rest of us, we screw up all the time. It's called being human. Look, you can find girls like me all over Manhattan and L.A. But girls like Kelly...she's the kindest, most loving person I've ever known. She's too trusting, and her record with awful men is appalling. Turns out you're no different than the rest of them."

"She lied to me over and over again."

Mimi pursed her lips as if she were concentrating. "My guess is, it wasn't so much to protect herself, but you. She was worried about your health and didn't want to cause you any undue pain. Knowing her, she probably thought you'd hang around a few weeks, she'd nurse you back to health, and you'd be on your way never the wiser. But then she fell for you, and she found herself in a quandary."

"How do you know?" Rafe asked, skeptical.

"What?"

"That she really fell for me. It was all a lie."

Mimi shook her head in disgust. "Did you see her face when you left? I've just discovered that over the last couple of weeks she'd left me five million messages asking me what she should do about you. She told me about the subterfuge and that she wasn't sure how to tell you the truth. And she was right—you did lose your cool and run away. As far as I'm concerned, she's an idiot for falling for you in the first place."

Eyes narrowing, he glared at her sister. It wasn't that she was shallow, but her casual dismissal of her sister's pain seemed callous. What had he ever found so attractive about her?

"Well, here you are." Mimi pointed out the window to the airport. "When you do figure out what a moron you've been, don't bother writing. I'm going to make sure my sister never has to see or hear from you again. You don't deserve her. She's way too good for you."

The driver opened the door and Rafe eased himself out of the vehicle. Before he knew it, the taxi was gone.

This was it.

In a few hours, he would be thousands of miles away from the island and Kelly's lies.

He had to leave, to sort out his own life, make the right choices for him without worrying about anyone else.

The memory of her beautiful face stained with tears haunted him.

No. He would do this. He needed a clean break.

That's what he wanted, right?

19

"HE'S GONE," KELLY told her parents.

Her father went to her right away and put his arm around her shoulder.

"This is what happens when you aren't honest with the people you love. I'm no better than you and Mom."

Her father harrumphed but just squeezed her tighter.

Her mother touched her back affectionately. "That man will realize how much he loves you and return on his knees. Men can be a bit slow sometimes."

Ignoring his wife, her father guided her to the couch.

"Do you love him?" he asked.

"Dad, that's personal."

Her mother handed her a tissue and she held it to her nose.

"Yes, it is," he said, "but you need to say it out loud."

"I love him, more than anything. But he left. The thing is, I was surprised that he left. Some small part of me hoped he would understand. That what I did wasn't as selfish as it seemed. I never meant to hurt him."

"You did, though," Mimi countered as she strutted

into the room. "He's mad. I tried to talk to him, but he wouldn't listen."

"Mimi, you probably made it worse." Kelly closed her eyes. Why couldn't they just leave her alone?

Her sister thumped her on the head. "It couldn't get much worse."

"Mimi! This isn't the time," her mother admonished.

Kelly was ready to scream about the insensitivity of her sister, but she remembered this had all started because she'd pretended to be her.

"He was furious, which means he cares—a lot. Really, you think you'd know something about men by now." She rolled her eyes. Then she sat down next to Kelly. "Listen to your big sister for once. He'll be back."

"Mimi, I can't believe you interfered. Things are bad enough without you nosing into my private life. That goes for all of you. None of you ever cared about who I was dating before. Why now?"

Mimi pulled on her pigtail. "Behave, brat. We love you. The man you love has strolled out the door, that's why we care. He'll remember why he adores you even more than you do him. He'd be a fool to walk away from the best thing that ever happened to him. Now, how fast that happens, I couldn't say. He's pretty hardheaded."

She had a point. "Do you really think he'll forgive me?"

Mimi scrunched up her nose. "From what I saw, once he realizes what he's missing, he'll be running back so fast it'll be like one of your tropical storms blew in."

"Speaking of which, that storm will probably be here in a couple of hours. We need to make sure all the beach chairs and things are collected and put in the shed." Work. She needed to work.

Her father kissed her forehead. "Don't worry, Kelly. We will take care of everything. Your staff is incredibly adept and most of it is already done."

Kelly jumped up. "It's a small front, it won't be that bad, but—Adrien!"

"*Ma petite,* what did I tell you about yelling? I am not deaf. What did you need?" He stopped short when he saw Mimi.

Mimi, in turn, frowned, her brow creasing.

Kelly and her mother stared back and forth from Mimi to Adrien and back again to Mimi.

"Um, the truck, Adrien," said Kelly. "We need to make sure it's full—"

"Seen to. The generators are also fueled and ready. Everything that can be boarded down has been. We have food and drink, enough to feed the island for a few days, if necessary. But all indications are that the storm's intensity is waning and that it will die out before it hits land."

Kelly stood with her hands on her hips. "Oh. Thanks. You didn't have to do all that."

"I'm a hired hand, that's what we do."

A hired hand? He was a world-renowned chef who loved to cook and surf. She noticed that Mimi had crossed her arms and was sitting on the sofa sulking.

"So, there's nothing left to do?" she asked.

"Your father and I will look after the last of the outdoor furniture and that's it," Adrien replied.

Kelly blew out a breath. "I'm feeling somewhat irrelevant."

"Oh, honey, you were so upset," her mother said. "We thought it best not to disturb you in your room."

She had been in there for a few hours. The tears just wouldn't seem to stop.

Rafe, I wish you could know how sorry I am. I love you so much.

Kelly couldn't even begin to hope. The look of anger and hurt on his face was something she would never forget. Her family was sweet to try to console her, but they didn't understand Rafe the way she did. The marine in him saw things in black-and-white, and he lived by a code. One that was about being honest and forthright. Protecting those who needed it. And she'd thrown it all away. "Oh, no, my necklace!"

She took off in search of the silver thread with the tiny surfboard attached. It was the last thing Rafe had given to her, and she'd dropped it on the beach somewhere.

There was no way he'd come back to her. The keepsake was all she'd ever have of him.

Her shattered soul broke into more pieces as her knees hit the sand.

"SIR, I'M SORRY. There's nothing we can do. The last flight took off fifteen minutes ago. You should have called before you arrived. The airport is closing. Tomorrow afternoon, if the planes are okay, will be the earliest we can get you over to the main island." The woman behind the desk at the ticket counter stared at him as if she'd heard it all and then some. He'd been at the end of a very long line of angry customers.

The marine in him forced a smile. "Understood. Can we go ahead and book a flight for tomorrow now?"

The relief on the poor woman's face was evident. "I can put your name on the list. They aren't allowing us

to book anything for the next twenty-four hours because
it depends on how the storm hits, and if the planes are
damaged. This happens often this time of year, when
the storms happen one after another."

Rafe took a long, steadying breath. "Okay."

"We do have rooms available at some of the hotels
nearby, though you may need to share with someone."

This just kept getting better and better. "Thanks, I'll
see what I can find on my own." He gave her a tight
smile and moved out of the way. It was as if the universe
had conspired against him. There was no way to get to
the mainland, no matter how badly he wanted to leave.

Rafe slung his sack over his shoulder and took a few
steps. What was he going to do? He didn't have anywhere to stay and he sure wasn't going to share a room
with a stranger.

Anger churned in his gut, and he considered putting
his fist through a wall. Trigger. Any kind of emotional
turmoil set him off—he'd talked about it with his doctors. At first, he'd had a difficult time seeing the signs,
but now he was aware of how it happened and why and,
more importantly, what to do about it.

A few months ago, the frustration and feelings of betrayal would have sent him off the edge. But he closed
his eyes and calmed his mind. Instead of hitting the
wall, he went to the men's room and splashed water on
his face. The cool water was welcome in the heat of the
muggy airport. The storm coming in had made the hu-
midity practically unbearable.

He considered his options. There weren't any rules
about not staying at the airport, and he'd slept in worse
places. He'd find a corner and shut his eyes.

As if that were possible.

Why had Kelly lied to him? None of it made sense. She should have been straight from the beginning.

Thinking about her betrayal wasn't helping anything. He was disappointed because he thought they might have found something special. He'd never had that kind of connection with a woman. From that first moment on the driveway, she'd stolen his breath—and his heart.

He'd come to Fiji expecting a weeklong fling with Mimi. In her place, he found the woman of his dreams, one who had made him think about his future. His was so uncertain, yet it was probably best that he leave.

She'd hurt him badly, and he'd lashed out. Well, he'd taken off. The same thing her dad did when he couldn't take what was going on with her mother. What had he said about marines never running away from trouble? They always ran toward it.

Rafe sat down in a quiet spot of the lobby and sagged against the wall.

So why didn't he stay and fight?

Because you're a coward. He recalled the night he and Kelly had first made love. She'd been trying to tell him something, but he'd suggested they leave the past behind them. Then she'd tried to talk to him again when they'd been interrupted by Mimi's arrival.

She'd been trying to tell him the truth.

The idea struck at him like a bomb, shattering his anger. It wasn't the night in New York that had attracted him to Mimi—it had been her letters.

Kelly's letters.

He had fallen for the woman who had written him every day, which had encouraged him, pushed him, supported him…the woman who had listened to his every complaint without judgment.

When he'd arrived in Fiji, Kelly had done nothing but help him heal his body and his soul. And she'd asked for nothing in return.

Yeah, she'd pretended to be her sister, but in name only. The words she'd sent, those were her words. The invitation was hers, too.

The wild attraction he felt for her wasn't some figment of his imagination—it was an extension of the feelings she'd already aroused with her letters. He'd been in love with Kelly before he ever got to the island. And he was fairly certain she felt the same way about him.

"I'm an idiot," he whispered.

"You'll get no argument here, son." Carter Callahan stood above him.

Rafe lifted his head. "Sir." He couldn't imagine why the man was there. Probably to give him a beating for hurting his daughter. And damned if Rafe didn't feel like he deserved it.

Carter held out a hand to help him up, and Rafe took it.

"I need your assistance with something," Carter said seriously.

Rafe frowned. "I'm not sure what I could do, sir, but I'll help if I can."

"Hoped you'd say that, soldier. Get your pack and let's go."

Used to taking orders, Rafe did as the man asked and followed him out of the airport.

"Thank God." Raina was at the wheel of an expensive SUV. "Adrien called—the swells are higher than expected and he still can't get her to move."

"What's going on? Who won't move?"

"Kelly," her mother said. "She's looking for something on the beach and, short of knocking her over the head and dragging her inside, we can't get her to move. She's soaking wet and going to catch pneumonia."

"Never seen her like this," Carter said.

"Why did you leave her?"

"Adrien and Mimi are trying to help her find whatever it is she lost. But it's getting dangerous out there."

Hell. What had he done?

"Kelly's a strong girl, but she's under a lot of stress. You hurt her, Rafe, and she's not thinking logically. We were hoping maybe you could tell us what she's looking for on the beach. And we thought, perhaps, if you don't mind, you could talk some sense into her."

He couldn't look at Kelly's parents. He'd put their daughter's life in danger because he'd run off like a rat.

He had to make it up to her, do whatever it took. He'd haul her over his shoulder if he had to and apologize until she forgave him.

The torrential rain and wind were so strong that he wasn't sure how Raina was keeping the car on the slick roads. Suddenly, the wind whipped up around them and he was sure the SUV would tumble onto its side.

"I want to be clear about this. We aren't asking you to do anything other than to convince her to come inside," Carter said. "The situation between you two, well, we're the last two to give advice about communication in a relationship."

"Besides, it's none of our business," Raina added.

He wished Kelly were around to hear that. No one would be more surprised than his surfer girl.

His girl.

Hell. If she was sick, or hurt, because of their fight, he would never forgive himself.

"If she'll have me back, I'll make it up to her," Rafe said, more to himself than to anyone.

"You better," Raina murmured.

Here he thought he was the brave one, but it was Kelly. She'd helped him move on from one of the worst times of his life with nothing but her generosity and her heart.

He had to get back to her.

He had to fix this.

A branch from a large palm tree flew past as Raina swerved into the resort's driveway.

"This storm has hit faster than the weatherman said it would," she said as she shifted into Park.

Rafe left his bag in the car and ran as fast as he could through the blinding rain. He didn't let himself slow down until he found her.

Adrien and Mimi both wore rain slickers, but Kelly was in shorts and a tank top, digging through the sand.

In spite of his leg aching from the run, he knelt down in front of her and grabbed her hands. She abruptly pulled away from him, never looking up.

"Kelly, whatever it is, we'll find it tomorrow," he said.

The wind blew hard and fast around them as thunder clapped and boomed in the distance. He had to get her into the mansion. The storm surge was closing in.

"I have to find it," she said, her voice low and harsh. "It's all I have left. The sea will take it, and I'll never have it again."

"Kelly! Look at me." He gently took her by the shoulders and made her face him.

"But you left," she whispered.

"Yes, I did. And it was one of the dumbest things I've ever done. Now come on, the storm is dangerous. You're going to get hurt out here."

She glanced around as if she'd just noticed the driving rain and dangerous waves heading their way. Rearing back from him, she stood and asked, "Why are you here?"

"Kelly, I'm sorry."

"No. You shouldn't have come back." Kelly ran for the sliding glass doors that led to her bedroom in the main house, her sister close on her heels. Rafe watched them through the raging storm.

Adrien offered Rafe a hand up. "Crap."

Rafe agreed, "You got that right. I'm in deep, brother, and it looks like I'm going to need one hell of a shovel."

20

KELLY WOKE IN her bed feeling stuffy and crowded. She blinked open her eyes to find her sister beside her. "What happened?" she asked, yawning.

Her brain felt as woolly as the jar of cotton balls she kept under her sink. She soon realized there was another body on the other side of her. Crowded, indeed. "Mom?"

"Morning, darling girls. Are you feeling better, Kelly?"

Her mother turned over and gave them a warm smile.

"I don't know what I am yet. Why are you two in my bed?"

"The condos at the other end of the beach were hit hard by the storm surge. They were trying to find places for people to stay and we took in about twenty. Lucky for us, the worst of it hit on the other side of the island. We lost electricity, but other than that we're good. The solar generators are running, so far so good."

Kelly, openmouthed, stared at her mother.

Her mom sat up. "What is it?"

There was a storm? Kelly must have been out of it completely. She forced her brain to go over the past twenty-four hours and she winced. "Was Rafe here?"

"Yep," replied Mimi as she got up and stood by the side of the bed. "I'll go check on the guests."

Kelly's face met her palm. "I ran away from him last night. Why did I do that? He probably thinks I'm ridiculous and a liar." Why couldn't she get it right just once? The universe had given her a second chance and she'd blown it.

Her mother watched her with a guarded look.

"He left, didn't he?" Kelly's heart squeezed tight.

"I honestly don't know. He and Adrien were helping with the relief efforts on the other side of the island. Your dad is there, too."

Kelly stared up at the ceiling. "I guess I'll have to learn to live with my mistakes. He'll probably have Adrien drop him off at the airport as soon as it opens."

"Kelly Callahan, you are not going to run away from this. You will fight for your marine with everything you are. Go find him, apologize again. And make him see what you mean to each other," her mother ordered.

Leaning over, she kissed her mother on the cheek. "I love you, mom. But I'm going to help Mimi with our guests."

She appreciated her mother's optimism, but Kelly lived in the real world. Her relationship with Rafe was over.

KELLY SAT ON the sand, staring out at the horizon. Her bright pink board was stuck upright beside her. The hunch in her shoulders spoke volumes.

"I'm pretty sure you have to put that thing in the water for it to work," Rafe joked as he sat down beside her.

Tears streaked her face, and the sight hit him hard.

So hard that he knew it was a sign of what he'd put her through and how much he genuinely regretted it.

"I'm sorry." It wasn't enough, but he had to try.

She continued staring out at the horizon, not even glancing in his direction.

"I overreacted and it kills me that I hurt you. I swear I'll never do it again."

Using the heel of her hand, she wiped her tears.

"There's no excuse for what I did," he said, desperate to get through to her. "I wanted to yell and I never yell. I was overwhelmed and confused. What you did was wrong, but I shouldn't have walked out."

He'd met her parents and recognized the abandonment. Her father always left her mother, and she'd grown up around that drama. Rafe had done the same thing to her.

"You don't need to apologize." She pulled her knees up and put her head on them. "You had a right to get mad. I deceived you, and even if I did it for a good reason, it was wrong."

He pulled her to him and she let him. "Kelly, tell me what I need to do to make this better."

"*You?* I'm the one who screwed up bad. I hope that someday you'll be able to forgive me."

Her head was down and he lifted her chin up to look into her eyes. "There's nothing to forgive, babe. I understand now why you did it. And it's just one of those things that got out of control. I've had a few of those situations in my life."

"Yeah? Well, I don't blame you for leaving. I lied to you. I manipulated you and before I could tell you the truth, you found out anyway. But you left. You left when I tried to tell you what happened. You assumed that I did it because I pity you and I will tell you right now, Rafe McCawley, the last thing I ever felt for you was pity."

"I've told you more than once what an idiot I am, and I've been kicking myself the entire way back here. Babe, please tell me that you aren't giving up on us. Things have moved fast between us, but we're good together. We had an argument, that's what people in love do. We made mistakes, but we can learn from those. Kelly, I love you so much."

He held his breath.

She shook her head. "It hurts too much. I can't lose you again, Rafe. I know you think I'm tough, but when it comes to you I'm not. It scares me how much I love you."

The declaration put fire into his resolve. He straightened up and gave her a hard look. She cared. She loved him. She didn't get to take that back.

"Listen to me, Kelly Callahan," Rafe said sternly. "You are tough, and anything that comes in the future, we will overcome it together. I can promise, with all that I am, that I will never run out on you again. You can trust me."

She eyed him carefully but didn't say anything. This wonderful woman cared for him and had helped him heal.

"I can't believe you came back."

"What are you talking about? I just went out for a little air," he joked.

"Um, Rafe."

"Yes, baby."

"Next time you go out for a little air, please don't break my heart and take it with you."

A direct hit.

"Kelly, that's the real reason I had to come back. I

knew I'd left my heart with you. We're a pair, you and I. You know it as well as I do."

She gave a shaky sigh. "I want to believe you."

"I love you, Kelly, and I'm giving you my word as a marine that I will spend the rest of my life making it up to you. And that my sole purpose will be to make you the happiest woman on the planet."

A hint of a smile quivered on her lips.

"What?" Rafe asked.

"I love you, too," she said softly.

Rafe let out a breath.

She bit her bottom lip. "And you're a good kisser. It's hard to find those these days. Trust me, I've been all over almost every continent, and you're definitely the best."

Relief eased the hurt in his soul. His Kelly was his again. "Wait a minute. I don't like the idea of you kissing so many men," he complained. "From now on it's just me. Got it?"

She gave him a fake salute. "Maybe you should remind me."

He didn't understand what she meant.

"About the kissing," she clarified.

He started feathering kisses on her forehead, down the side of her face and neck. Then he captured her sweet lips with his.

They did belong together. And he knew now that soul mates did exist. His was a beautiful blonde surfer who took his breath away.

After many minutes of reminding her how good a kisser he was, he stopped to gaze lovingly at this woman he adored.

"You are so beautiful," he whispered reverently.

She placed a hand on his chest where his heart was. "I still can't believe you're here."

He gave her his best, warmest smile. "I swear you are stuck with me. And think of the great story we'll have to tell our kids one day."

"Kids?" she squeaked.

"Yep. I'm thinking at least three or four, maybe twelve. We could have our own football and surf teams."

Her eyes flashed wide and her jaw dropped.

"Obviously, that's negotiable," he added as he kissed the tip of her nose. "Remember, when it comes to negotiating, name the terms you want."

"Do you have terms?"

"I'm accepting the honorable discharge I've been offered, so I'll be taking care of you from now on. No one is ever going to mess with you again. We'll make our dreams come true together. As for Last Resort, Adrien is more than willing to take over as assistant manager. I talked to him about this morning.

"Oh, and another one of my terms is marriage. You and me, a minister and a pair of rings. We don't have to do it now, but I want to make you mine. And I want everyone to know it. But until we can get the rings, I want you to wear this." He held up the silver necklace with the surfboard.

"You found it!"

No, but he would never tell her that. When she'd been so desperate the night before, it occurred to him what must have happened. She hadn't known that the necklace had been in his pocket the whole time. He'd gone back to the beach and picked it up off the sand before leaving for the airport.

"I think the universe wants you to have this." He put

it around her neck. "This is to remind you that the next time we argue, both of us are staying put. And that you belong to me."

She kissed him. "Boy, you sure are bossy. We're going to have kids and we're going to get married, and now I'm a possession." She pretended to talk like he did. "You've forgotten the most important thing."

"What?"

"The make-up sex. That's first. Then the rest of that stuff comes later."

They laughed. As he stood up, he playfully dumped her on the sand. Before she knew what was going on, he'd scooped her up and hoisted her over his shoulder.

She lost it in a fit of giggles. "Put me down, you gorilla," she said as she pounded her fists against his back.

"You're only turning me on more."

She giggled again.

"What is it?"

"I was just thinking about what it would be like to have a bunch of little Rafes running around. And here I thought this family was already out of control. Can you imagine?"

Rafe smiled.

Yes, he could imagine that and an entire life with her.

She was his surfer babe, and he was never going to let her go.

* * * * *

*Don't miss HER LAST BEST FLING,
Candace Havens's next sexy romance, involving
another hot marine who's met his match!
Available in November from Harlequin Blaze!*

REQUEST YOUR FREE BOOKS!
2 FREE NOVELS PLUS 2 FREE GIFTS!

HARLEQUIN®

Blaze®

red-hot reads!

SPECIAL EXCERPT FROM

 HARLEQUIN®

 *Blaze*®

Bestselling author Leslie Kelly is back
with *another* sizzling Forbidden Fantasy!

Lying in Your Arms

Available September 17, 2013,
wherever Harlequin books are sold.

Leo checked out the rest of the room, pausing in the bathroom to strip out of his clothes and grab a towel, which he slung over one shoulder. He returned to the patio door, put one hand on the jamb and another on the slider, and stood naked in the opening, letting that tropical breeze bathe his body in coolness.

Heaven.

He was just about to step outside and let the warm late-day sun soak into his skin when he heard something very out of place. A voice. A woman's voice. Coming from right behind him…inside his room.

"Oh. My. God!"

Shocked, he swung around, instinctively yanking the towel off his shoulder.

A woman stood in his room, staring at him, wide-eyed. They stared at each other, silent, surprised, and Leo immediately noticed several things about her.

She was young—his age, maybe. Definitely not thirty.

She was uncomfortable, tired or not feeling well. Her blouse clung to her curvy body, as it was moist with sweat.

HBEXP79771

Dark smudges cupped her red-rimmed eyes, and she'd already kicked off her shoes, which rested on the floor right by the door, as if her first desire was to get barefoot, pronto.

Oh. And she was hot. Jesus, was she ever.

She was one more thing, he suddenly realized.

Shocked. Stunned. Maybe a little afraid.

"Hi," he said with a small smile. He remained where he was, not wanting to startle her.

Her green eyes moved as she shifted her attention over his body, from bare shoulders, down his chest, then toward the white towel that he clutched in his fist right at his belly. Finally, something like comprehension washed over her face.

"Look, I don't know who put you up to this, but I don't need you."

"Don't need me for what?" *To do your taxes? Cut your hair? Carry your suitcase?*

Put out your fire?

Oh, he suspected he could do that last one, and it wasn't just because of his job.

"To have sex with me."

His jaw fell open. *"What?"*

She licked her lips. "I mean, you're very attractive and all." Her gaze dropped again. "Still, I think you'd better get out."

"I can't do that," he said, his voice low, thick.

He edged closer, unable to resist lifting a hand to brush a long, drooping curl back from her face, tucking it behind her ear.

"Why not?" she whispered.

"Because you're in my room."

**Pick up LYING IN YOUR ARMS by Leslie Kelly,
on sale September 17, 2013,
wherever Harlequin® Blaze® books are sold.**

Every bachelorette party has a surprise...

And for Angie Lawson it's seeing her ex-boyfriend at a strip club, standing right in front of her—every sexy, delicious inch of him. Cole Foster isn't the kind of guy that *any* woman can just ignore....

Cole's working undercover and needs Angie's help to get into the bridal party. And if getting there means getting her in bed, too, then he's *definitely* the best man for the job!

Pick up

The Bridesmaid's Best Man

by *Susanna Carr,*

available September 17, 2013, wherever you buy Harlequin Blaze books.

H HARLEQUIN®

Blaze®

Red-Hot Reads
www.Harlequin.com

Mission: Keep Margaret Barlow distracted...using any means necessary!

All professor Maggie Barlow wanted was a night of wicked satisfaction from the dead-sexy ranger, Hunter Cross. Having him as her official army liaison while she works on her new book? That *wasn't* in the plan. Especially when she learns that Hunter has orders to "control" her. Little does the army know that when it comes to their deliciously naughty nighttime activities, Hunter is at Maggie's complete command....

Pick up

Command Performance

by *Sara Jane Stone,*

available September 17, 2013, wherever you buy Harlequin Blaze books.

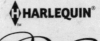

Red-Hot Reads
www.Harlequin.com

HB79774

HARLEQUIN®

A Romance FOR EVERY MOOD™

Love the Harlequin book you just read?

Your opinion matters.

Review this book on your favorite book site, review site, blog or your own social media properties and share your opinion with other readers!

Be sure to connect with us at:
Harlequin.com/Newsletters
Facebook.com/HarlequinBooks
Twitter.com/HarlequinBooks

HARLEQUIN®

A *Romance* FOR EVERY MOOD™

**Stay up-to-date on all your
romance-reading news with the
Harlequin Shopping Guide,
featuring bestselling authors, exciting new
miniseries, books to watch and more!**

The newest issue will be delivered right to you
with our compliments! There are 4 each year.

Signing up is easy.

EMAIL

ShoppingGuide@Harlequin.ca

WRITE TO US

HARLEQUIN BOOKS
Attention: Customer Service Department
P.O. Box 9057, Buffalo, NY 14269-9057

OR PHONE

1-800-873-8635 in the United States
1-888-343-9777 in Canada

Please allow 4-6 weeks for delivery of the first issue by mail.